Irene Morck

Irene Morck was born in St. John, New Brunswick, but has spent much of her life on the prairies, apart from two years in Barbados and ten years in Jamaica, where she taught chemistry at a boy's school and did research in biochemistry at the University of the West Indies.

Since 1979, she has lived on a farm near Spruce View, Alberta, with her husband, Mogens Nielsen. Together they raise hay and grain and enjoy such hobbies as trail riding, photography, canoeing, cross country skiing, learning Spanish and traveling. They have no children, but do have lots of animals — cattle, horses, mules, cats, a dog and a singing canary.

Irene has written numerous articles for syndicates and magazines in the United States and Canada. Her first novel, *A Question of Courage*, was a Canadian Children's Book Centre "Our Choice" selection and was nominated for several major awards. Her work has been translated into Danish and French.

As the eldest of seven children, Irene knows all about the problem of siblings at war.

BETWEEN BROTHERS

BETWEEN BROTHERS

IRENE MORCK

Stoddart

AN IRWIN YOUNG ADULT BOOK

Published in 1992 by
Stoddart Publishing Co. Limited
34 Lesmill Road
Toronto, Canada
M3B 2T6

Canadian Cataloguing in Publication Data

Morck, Irene
Between brothers

ISBN 0-7773-5530-6

(Irwin young adult fiction)

I. Title   II. Series

PS8576.0628B48 1992   jC813'.54   C92-094798-0
PZ7.M672Be 1992

Cover design: Brant Cowie/ArtPlus
Cover illustration: David Craig
Typesetting: Tony Gordon Ltd.

Printed and bound in Canada

*Stoddart Publishing gratefully acknowledges the support of the
Canada Council, Ontario Arts Council and Ontario Publishing Centre
in the development of writing and publishing in Canada.*

For my husband and my mother,
For my sisters and my brothers,
and to each person who, by believing in me,
helped make this book.

BETWEEN BROTHERS

One

"**B**ut, Dad, I just can't miss this party!" I said, struggling not to yell in front of Ken, Janice and Amanda — especially Amanda. My friends had always seen me as Mr. Cool, in control of every situation. Yet here I was almost losing it while they sat rigid on the couch, eyes narrowed, watching the rest of us.

I took a deep breath. "It's all Michael's fault. He's the absentminded genius who lost Holly Wilson's horse when you guys were trail riding. There's no way I should have to miss Amanda's sixteenth birthday party and spend a week getting saddle sores."

My father clenched his grubby hands. "Greg, we have to go back out to the mountains tomorrow, and Holly has to come along to catch that horse. So we need two trailers to carry enough animals for riding and packing. Mr. Wilson can't go, and there's nobody else to drive his truck."

I glared at Michael, but for once my younger brother wasn't saying anything, which made me even angrier.

Plastering a smile across my face, I turned to my friends. "Would you believe this brother of mine turned sixteen over two months ago and he still hasn't bothered to take his driver's test?"

My friends snickered. Their eyes darted from Dad and Michael back to me, like spectators at a tennis match. Then we all stared at Dad and Michael again. It was disgraceful for a university professor, or even his son, to look and smell so terrible. This was Friday, the day they were due back from their week in the mountains, but I thought they'd be home and showered long before Ken and the two girls came over to start taping music for the party. Who could have dreamed that the great trail riders would come tramping in at ten o'clock at night and cause such a scene in front of my friends.

"Greg, we need you to drive that truck," my father said again.

I looked at Mom, lifting my hands in exasperation. "This is Michael's problem, not mine. He always messes everything up —"

"Greg, that's enough," Dad said.

I gulped. "Dad, this is the biggest party of the year. And I *have* to help."

My father's jaw set. "You can finish taping the music tomorrow morning while Michael and I get everything ready."

"It isn't just the music, Professor Kepler." Janice cracked her chewing gum and looked through long eyelashes. "It's the planning and the decorating —"

"And the party itself," Amanda said, her voice sharp. "Greg, we need you at the party."

Ken poked Amanda in the ribs and drawled under his breath, "The guy's almost old enough to vote . . ."

"Excuse me!" Mom's eyes flashed. "Greg, we'll discuss this later."

"There really isn't anything to discuss," I said, not even daring to look at my friends, fighting to regain control of my voice. I'd die, literally die, if I lost face in front of them.

"Greg, I'm sure we'll get you back in time for your party next Friday," Dad said. "Who knows, we might find the horse right away."

"But what if we don't?" I took another deep breath. "I'll bet whether or not we found him we'd come home in time for you to start teaching summer school."

"We'll discuss this later," Dad said.

"Come on, let's go," Amanda said. "I can tell when we aren't wanted."

Ken scowled. "Yeah." He slapped me on the back as he walked toward the door. "Well, cowboy, we'll see you tomorrow. But then again, maybe we won't. Who knows, Kepler, you might enjoy a week in the mountains with Holly Wilson." He laughed coarsely.

Amanda and Janice giggled.

I gritted my teeth. "Don't worry," I said, trying to pull my face into a smile, "I'll be here to help with the party."

The minute Ken and the others were out the door, I shook my fist at Michael. "You idiot! How come you can remember every stupid word Shakespeare ever wrote and the Latin name of every dumb plant or animal that ever lived, but you can't remember anything important? How could you forget to hobble Holly Wilson's horse?"

Again, Michael didn't answer and that made me furious.

"Was it really asking too much," I sneered, "for your brilliant brain to remember to buckle a couple of leather straps around one horse's front feet so he couldn't run off into the wild blue yonder?"

Michael sat silent, his head bent as though I were hitting him.

Mom turned to Dad. "Can't you and Michael figure out some way of getting back out there by yourselves?" she asked. "Greg has been looking forward to Amanda's party for weeks. And you know how much he hates camping and riding horses. Surely his feelings count for something."

Dad shook his head. "The horses can't all fit in one trailer." Once my Dad had decided something, it was just about impossible to make him back down. You could yell and scream about it all you wanted. He wouldn't budge. But Mom and I never learned.

She put her hands on her hips. "It's hard to believe that a big important oil executive like Sheldon Wilson can't find somebody to drive his truck, someone who would be just thrilled to ride up and down the mountains next week looking for a lost horse."

Dad frowned. "He has to fly to Texas tomorrow. He doesn't have time to start phoning around."

"He could find somebody!" Mom was almost shouting now. "It's his daughter's horse!"

"But we're responsible for losing him. I told you, Sheldon was chopping wood —"

"Yeah, I know, I know. You and Michael were supposed to bring the horses in from grazing and tie them for the night. But if Sheldon knows that Patches pulls back, he should have reminded you to hobble him."

"He did remind me," Michael said quietly. Those were the first words he'd spoken during the whole argument.

As usual Dad stepped in. "It was my fault, too," he said. "I shouldn't have left Michael to bring in the last couple of horses alone. If I hadn't decided I just had to have a walk before dark, it never would have happened. So it's our responsibility to find that horse. Sheldon Wilson had absolutely nothing to do with losing it."

"Neither did I!" I shouted. "And I'm not going out there to look for it."

* * *

I pressed the gas pedal to the floor and leaned against the blue velvet seat of Mr. Wilson's dual-wheel crew cab truck.

Holly Wilson stiffened as I shifted into a lower gear and roared the truck up the steep graveled road. "Greg Kepler," she said, looking at me sideways through the edge of her thick glasses, "It's good my dad isn't here to see the way you're driving his pride and joy."

I snorted. "If your dad were here, I'd be in Calgary enjoying myself this week."

Ahead of us the brake lights of my father's truck and trailer flashed a few times, an eerie red pulsing through the thick cloud of dust behind him. This was Dad's way of telling me he thought I was following too close. He didn't like to make a truck work for him up a steep hill.

He always had to take everything nice and easy. Just like Michael. The two of them were probably having a great time up there, talking and laughing.

I turned my head from the road for a moment to glare at Holly. "Do you really think you're going to find your horse?"

She didn't hesitate. "We have to."

"What if we don't?"

Out of the corner of my eye I could see her chin jut. "We are going to find him, Greg."

This was Saturday night. Six more days until my party. And the next Monday morning Dad would be starting his Education Methods classes for a bunch of middle-aged teachers.

Some day Holly would probably be a middle-aged teacher taking summer-school courses. "Thick" was the word you'd use to describe her. Thick glasses. Thick short brown hair. Thick short body. Thick arms and legs. Not fat. Just kind of thick. Certainly not the type of girl I hung around.

When a girl sat far away from a guy in a vehicle, my friends said she was "polishing the door handle." Well, after three hours of driving with me from Calgary, Holly had that door handle real shiny.

Even if we did make it back in time for the party, it really burned me up to think that I had to waste any of my precious summer riding horses all over the mountains with my father, my brother and a girl like Holly just because I had a driver's license.

I turned the radio louder, much louder, glancing at Holly. She stiffened even more. Obviously she didn't share my taste in music. It was hard to believe that

Holly was only sixteen. She seemed more like forty-five. I thought of Amanda and all the other gorgeous girls who had snuggled up against me in my beautiful old red Mustang, cruising the streets of Calgary, and I sighed.

I looked at my watch. Six o'clock. For sure Mom would be home from the office by now. Lately it seemed she was spending all her Saturdays working. Mom was lucky she didn't have to go on this ridiculous expedition. Horseback riding and camping weren't her idea of a good time either.

Six o'clock. No wonder I was hungry. Dad and Michael had taken the whole morning to wash their dirty clothes and buy groceries for the coming week. Then it took ages to load everything into the two trucks. We hadn't even left Calgary until the middle of the afternoon.

In mid-July in Alberta, it didn't get totally dark until well after nine o'clock, so we had lots of time to eat and put up the tent. Just thinking about having to sleep on the ground for a week made me groan.

The gravel road became much rougher. We were soon riding over ruts that would have hidden a dog. Holly's dad had bought this fabulous truck for the sole purpose of dragging his horses out here over rutty mountain roads. Big oil executives had money to burn, but it still didn't seem right to waste such a beautiful vehicle on roads like this.

We rounded a corner and my mouth gaped at the sight of more than two dozen truck-and-trailer outfits parked together in the middle of nowhere.

As soon as I pulled up beside Dad's truck, Holly

jumped out. Michael wandered back to Dad's trailer and stood, dazed as usual, staring in at the horses. Then he and Dad smiled broadly at each other. Real chummy, those two. It was enough to make a guy sick.

Michael was a photocopy of Dad, tall and skinny, with gray-blue eyes and plain brown hair. Nobody had ever raved about how Michael looked. Even when I was a little kid, old ladies had always gushed over me, saying I had Mom's good looks, especially her glossy black hair and huge brown eyes.

I climbed out of the truck. "Who belongs to all these vehicles?"

Dad laughed. "Lots of people. Mr. Wilson and Michael and I aren't the only ones crazy enough to go trail riding."

"Unbelievable." I shook my head.

Dad grinned and pointed toward the forest. "The river's just over there. This is called a staging area because the road ends here." It wasn't hard to tell that my father was a university professor. He was always explaining things to people.

"Staging area. That's a stupid name," I said.

"Might be, but that's what they call any place you start riding from." Stretching his arms, he sighed. "Smell that air. It feels great to be out here again! It's almost enough to make me glad that Michael forgot to hobble Patches." He pretended to duck. "Sorry, Holly. I didn't mean that."

Holly hadn't moved. She stared at the ground.

"Don't worry, we'll find your horse," Dad said. "Tell you what, let's go talk to those two guys over there. You never know, they might have seen him."

"Maybe we should unload the horses first," Michael said. "They must be tired of standing in the trailers."

I scowled at him. "They've stood in there for almost four hours. I'm sure another two minutes won't hurt them."

"Besides," Dad said, "those guys are just about ready to load their horses and drive out. We'd better get over there."

Two

*T*he two men glanced up as we approached. It was hard not to stare at their rumpled filthy clothes, blackened hands and dirty hair.

Dad spoke first. "I don't suppose either of you have seen a pinto out in those mountains anywhere?"

The younger guy answered. "We saw a few pintos. There's lots of people out there with lots of horses."

Holly said, "It's my horse . . ."

"How did you manage to lose him, girl?" the old guy drawled.

"Not me," Holly said. "I wasn't even along —"

Dad interrupted. "It happened Wednesday. During the night this pinto pulled back and broke the clip of his halter rope. We found him the next morning, but he wouldn't let us catch him. After a while he galloped into the forest and we couldn't find him again."

"Where did all this happen?" the older guy asked.

"North of Forbidden Valley. Up at Sky Lake."

The man whistled. "Wow. He could be anywhere by now."

Dad nodded. "We looked for him all day Thursday and all of yesterday morning, but then we had to pack up and drive back to Calgary last night."

"Because Holly's dad had to fly to Texas today for a week of meetings," Michael said.

"Why would they care about that?" I asked, embarrassed.

Michael looked at the ground. "I just thought —"

"You never think," I said, trying to keep my voice light.

"Greg!" Dad growled.

"Quite a few people lose their horses," said the younger guy, kicking a piece of gravel with his boot. "Some find them. Some don't. They say most wild horses in the mountains are really just animals that got away from their owners."

The other man lit a cigarette. "I knew a guy who looked a whole week for his horse and finally found her standing in some trees just about where she'd made her getaway. Blasted animal had probably been standing there, hiding behind the branches, laughing at him the entire time."

The younger man chuckled. "At least you guys have one thing going for you if he's hard to catch. You don't have to worry about anybody stealing him."

The older guy flicked his cigarette. "I never could stomach a horse that's hard to catch."

Holly clenched her teeth. "I can always catch him. Without oats, too. He just doesn't let anybody else catch him."

The man took off his grubby hat and wiped his forehead with an even grubbier hand. "If you've got a horse out in the mountains that's hard to catch or pulls back, you should always hobble him when he's tied."

"Yeah," I muttered to Holly. "Too bad Michael can't remember anything . . ."

The old guy cleared his throat. Dad glared at me, then turned back to the two men and said, "Well, I guess we'd better get our horses unloaded."

"We should be going too," said the other man. "It's a long drive home. Good luck, fellas."

We followed Dad back to our trucks. The two men loaded their animals and waved to us as they drove out.

Without a word, Michael opened our trailer door and disappeared among the horses. The metal clanged and banged as he backed out his flashy palomino, Lightning. After he tied Lightning to a tree, Michael stood with his face pressed against the horse's head, still not talking.

Dad backed out Muggs, his favorite horse. I never understood how Dad could like a horse with such an enormous ugly head. I figured that if you had to have a horse, you might as well have a beauty. This mare sure wasn't that.

Two men and two women came riding across the river leading three sweaty tired packhorses. They stopped and dismounted to talk to us. Yes, they'd had a great week. No, they hadn't seen Patches.

Over at the other side of the staging area, the four of them flung their saddles, blankets and pack boxes into two trucks. Within minutes they had the horses loaded and were driving out, trailers bouncing over the rough road.

Now we had the staging area to ourselves. Ourselves and about two dozen empty trucks and trailers.

Holly unloaded her mother's little brown gelding, Lucky. I watched as she tied him to a tree. That was the horse I was supposed to ride this week. Lucky. Lucky me.

The trailer clanged as Holly backed out Smoky, her dad's big gray riding horse. We'd be packing him this week. Next came Ginger, Mr. Wilson's gentle potbellied packhorse. Dad always said that a good packhorse had to have a potbelly to keep the two cinches in place.

Four horses to ride, three horses to pack. And, I sure hoped there'd soon be an eighth to haul back to Calgary.

When Holly unloaded the next horse, the animal spun around and almost fell out of the trailer. Holly yanked on his halter rope. "Bud, behave yourself." The golden-brown gelding reared as she tied him to a tree.

"You're gonna ride that crazy horse?" I asked.

"I'm used to him," she said. "Bud's always like this. Mom and Dad want to sell him. Sometimes I think they're right. He might never smarten up." Bud stood quivering, his nostrils flaring. "It's sure hard to believe," she added, "that our quiet peaceful Ginger gave birth to this crazy beast."

Dad was unloading Duke, the big brown gelding that Michael had ridden when he was younger. For the past couple of years Duke had been relegated to the job of carrying a pack. Dad and Mr. Wilson loved to argue about which was the best packhorse in the world, Duke or Ginger.

Dad slammed the trailer doors shut. "Now, we'd better put the tent up."

"What about supper?" I asked. "I'm starving."

"Me too," Michael chimed in. "I'll die if we don't eat pretty soon."

Dad laughed. "When Michael and Greg agree on something, we'd better do it."

Holly said, "Count me in. If we had to put the tent up before supper, I'd be chewing on the canvas."

Dad set his little propane camp stove on the ground. Starting tomorrow it would be just wood fires for heating water and for cooking. There wouldn't be room on any of our packhorses for such a luxury as a propane stove. So we'd be chopping down dead trees for firewood. Real fun.

Michael knelt to open a couple of cans of stew and dump them into the dented old cooking pot. While he was stirring the stew, he looked up at Holly and cackled, "'Double, double toil and trouble.'" Even I knew that's what the three witches in *Macbeth* chant while they're stirring their big stew pot, but I winced. It wasn't natural for a sixteen-year-old guy to go around quoting Shakespeare.

Holly laughed and finished the quote. "'Fire burn and cauldron bubble!'" Oh, boy. This was going to be quite a week stuck with not one, but two weirdos.

The smell of stew heating was torture to my hungry stomach, but finally supper was ready. Before Dad started eating, he filled a metal dishpan with water and put it on the stove to heat.

For dessert we each had an orange. I noticed that Dad and Michael had brought four bags of oranges. About the only thing Michael and I had in common was our passion for oranges. Each of us usually ate two or three a day.

While Dad washed the dishes, Holly and I dried them, and Michael tossed everything back into the pack boxes, jamming dishes and food in all over each other. I looked the other way. Messes bugged me.

"You guys sure brought lots of groceries," Holly said.

"We always do." My father was scrubbing dried crusted stew off the cooking pot. "Ever since the time it rained so hard your dad and I were trapped behind that flooded river. A few days of going hungry like that, and we vowed to always bring extra food."

"Too bad." Holly laughed and patted her hips. "I could lose some weight, you know."

Michael peered at her sideways. "Maybe that's why Patches has such a swayback."

"Yeah." Dad laughed. "Poor horse. Probably that's why he ran off. He thought he'd better make his get-away before you *broke* his back!"

Holly snapped her dish towel at them, but she was grinning from ear to ear. I was amazed. The girls I went around with were as thin as fashion models, but would have killed anyone who dared tease them about being even one bit overweight.

The sun was getting lower as Dad dumped the water out of the dishpan. "We'd better put that tent up now," he said.

Struggling under its bulky weight, we carried the

huge canvas tent to a grassy spot between the trees, almost tripping over some old spruce poles left by other campers. We'd need those poles, a long thick one for a ridgepole, to hold up the whole center length of canvas, and smaller poles for an A-frame support at each end. Holly and I helped Dad spread out the tent, which was as big as a cabin.

We tied the tent's many little top cords all along the ridgepole and, with rope, lashed together four smaller poles to make the A-frames. The sun had set and Dad turned on the headlights of both trucks so we could see better. Working within two overlapping sets of lights felt creepy, because long double shadows followed every move we made. Then we tried to erect the tent, fighting the weight of spruce poles and heavy canvas.

"Where's that lazy Michael?" I asked, my muscles straining.

"I'm feeding the horses."

I looked up. He had already piled hay in front of most of them and was hugging Lightning. "Get over here and do something worthwhile," I said.

"They're hungry." He picked up a big wad of hay to carry to the rest of the horses. "We had our supper. Why should they wait so long for theirs?"

"Get over here."

Flinging the hay on the ground, he strode toward me and grabbed the end of the ridgepole out of my hands.

I yanked it back. "Take one of the supports. Help Holly with that pole."

He grabbed the A-frame, almost knocking Holly's glasses off.

"Hey, watch it!" I yelled. "You trying to kill her?"

His eyes narrowed. "Since when is Greg Kepler concerned about anybody's welfare?"

"What's that supposed to mean?"

"You didn't have to put me down in front of those two men," Michael muttered as he lifted the A-frame.

"Then you shouldn't always act so dumb."

"It sure is going to be fun having you around this week," said my brother.

"You wouldn't have to have me around this week if you'd learned how to drive."

"Just because you got your license the minute you turned sixteen doesn't mean that everybody else has to. Some people have better things to do."

"Yeah, like wandering around in a daze."

"It's better than wandering around with stupid friends like yours."

"Cut it out, both of you." Dad grabbed the tent's front corner ropes and anchored them around a couple of trees. "Okay, you can let go. Do you guys know how awful I feel when you fight?"

Michael's lip pouted, shadowed grotesquely by the truck's headlights. "Do you know how awful I feel when Greg puts me down in front of strangers?"

By the time we rolled out our foam mats and sleeping bags, the silence between Michael and me was as cold as the night air. Summer evenings were certainly cooler in the mountains than in Calgary. We crawled into our sleeping bags fully clothed. I kept my jacket on too.

For an hour or more, I lay awake listening to Dad's snoring, Holly's soft regular breathing and the sound of seven horses munching hay just outside our tent.

Tonight a bunch of my friends would have started

making party decorations, laughing, listening to music, having a great time together. Just thinking about it hurt as though someone had kicked me in the stomach. Why did I have to have Michael for a brother?

In Calgary it wasn't so bad. We were apart at school all day. The rest of the time Michael was usually at Wilson's acreage, where Dad kept the horses, and I'd be out in my car with my friends. Even when we were at home at the same time, Michael usually had his nose in a book. Besides, we could always retreat into our own separate rooms if things got too tense between us.

Out here we'd have to be together twenty-four hours a day. It was starting to scare me.

Three

The delicious smell of fried bacon woke me. I looked at my watch. Only eight o'clock! Mighty kind of them to let me sleep in.

My back felt stiff. Why did people go to all this trouble to sleep on the cold ground when they could be home in a nice comfortable bed? I shivered. Boy, would a hot shower ever have felt good!

When I emerged from the tent, Dad was cooking pancakes. "Good *afternoon*, Greg!" He grinned and waved the spatula.

Holly said hi to me as she rooted around in the pack boxes. "I can't find any syrup," she mumbled.

Dad looked up. "We brought five bottles."

"Five bottles? For one week?"

"Yeah, Michael likes a few pancakes with his syrup."

Michael was nowhere in sight. Holly went back to rooting around in the boxes.

A couple of minutes later my brother appeared from the riverbank carrying two pails, sloshing water down the sides of his boots. As he set the pails on the ground he glanced at me, mumbled, "Hi," and walked toward the horses. They were all fed and brushed. He had probably been up for hours.

"Eureka!" Holly held two bottles of syrup above her head as though they were trophies. Michael smiled at her. He looked tired. No matter how late Michael went to bed, he was always awake at the first ray of morning light. My father and brother loved to get an early start on everything.

Dad was a good cook but I wasn't very hungry. I took an egg, a pancake and a piece of bacon.

"Greg, you'd better eat more than that," Dad said. "We won't be having lunch. It's hard to stop with packhorses. It'll take us a couple of hours to pack up, but it's only a three-hour ride into where we'll camp at Forbidden Valley, so we'll just keep going and have an early supper tonight."

I took another two pancakes but had a hard time choking them down. Michael devoured three fried eggs, about a dozen pieces of bacon and six big pancakes, drowning everything in syrup. He could eat the most fattening foods and never put on weight. He jogged every day but never put on any muscle, either.

Holly's eyebrows lifted as Michael reached for more pancake syrup. "Wow!" she said. "Maybe we should have brought ten bottles."

After we did the breakfast dishes, we took down the tent. Michael helped without being asked, avoiding my eyes.

Dad looked around. "Michael and I can do the packhorses. Holly, you get the saddle horses ready." He looked at me. "Greg, you can organize the pack boxes. Make sure they're weighted exactly the same, pair by pair and end for end."

I scowled. A seventeen-year-old shouldn't be bossed around like a little kid.

Dad smiled, totally ignoring my scowl. "And put the eggs in Duke's boxes. We don't want even one egg broken." He winked at Holly. "Not that I don't trust Ginger, but there's just no packhorse like Duke." He scratched Duke's face and the horse leaned against him. "Smooth, fast-walking, dependable, that's you, isn't it, old guy?"

Dad and Michael started putting the thick pads and pack saddles on Smoky, Duke and Ginger.

It was hard to believe that so much stuff could be packed on three horses. The huge tent, four sleeping bags, foam rubber mats, cooking pots, dishes, two dishpans, plastic ice-cream pails for carrying water, a bag of oats, our clothes, all the food . . .

"Do we really need to bring this much food along?" I asked. "It's enough for a month."

Dad smirked. "Not when we have old Hollow Legs with us."

The wooden pack boxes were about the size of a regular suitcase, but with the lid on one of the narrow sides. All the food and loose things had to fit in six boxes, one pair for each packhorse. Only the tent, foam mats, duffel bags and sleeping bags could be tied between the boxes as the "top pack."

The two metal dishpans stacked one inside the other. I stuffed them with groceries, slid the whole thing into a box, and packed more groceries around the sides. The plastic pails, stacked and filled with groceries, fit into a second box. As I crammed the first pair of boxes full, I kept lifting them to compare their weights. Finally I was sure they balanced perfectly. They were so heavy. Horses must be really stupid to carry all this weight around without protesting.

"Your first set is ready," I said.

Dad lifted one box, then the other, closing his eyes. "Nope, this one's too heavy on that end."

My stomach tightened. "They feel equal to me."

"The two boxes have to be exactly the same, Greg. Not just with each other, but end for end. Otherwise they start tipping to one side or to one end, and then a few minutes later everybody has to stop and wait while we repack. Hand me that can of tomatoes."

I watched while he stuffed the can into one corner, then lifted both boxes again, one at a time, his eyes closed, his brow furrowed. "Good. Now you feel them. That's the way they should be."

With a red face, I bent to lift the boxes. "Close your eyes," Dad said, "and swing them gently, up and down, side to side, and back and forth. That way you can tell if they're even a bit different."

Michael and Dad each waddled off with one of the finished boxes and I turned to work on the next pair. This set was going to be perfect. A few minutes later I looked up and saw Dad and Michael packing Ginger. They had already suspended the boxes, one on each side, in the loops of rope hanging from the wooden-framed pack saddle.

"Just a minute," I called. "I thought you were loading Duke first. Those were his boxes. With the eggs."

"It's okay. They can stay on Ginger. She's a pretty good packhorse, too." Dad turned to Holly. "Don't tell your dad I said that."

Sitting back on my heels, I watched Dad and Michael pack Ginger. A precision team, they made a couple of knots, threw the tent and two rolled foam mats on top of the boxes, spread a blue plastic tarp over the whole contraption, then tied a diamond hitch knot that would keep it all together. Michael seemed so competent out here, completely different from the way he was in the city. Too bad something couldn't be done about his forgetfulness.

After they tied the ax and the saw on top of Ginger's pack, Dad came over to test my next set of boxes. I watched carefully to see his reaction. I knew this pair was perfect. My father's eyes widened, then he grinned and bowed to me. "Well done, sir," he said.

I turned with more enthusiasm to my final set. Everything left had to fit on Smoky. When I had his boxes just about full, I picked up the pancake turner. What to do with such a long odd-shaped thing?

Dad and Michael had almost finished packing Duke. Strange. For such an experienced packhorse, he was acting tense and ill at ease, swishing his tail, stepping sideways. "Stand still, Duke," Dad ordered. "What's wrong with you?" They lifted the tarp over his pack and tied the diamond hitch. All that was left was to tighten the knot.

From my position on the ground I could see the underside of Duke's belly, and suddenly I realized that his hind cinch was too far back, almost into his flanks. That was how you made a rodeo horse buck.

"Hey, Dad!" I yelled. But just then he pulled hard on the rope and Duke erupted.

The horse lurched forward, put his head down and bucked. The top pack tipped to one side. He bucked again, harder, and it fell, bouncing out of the way. The boxes came loose and struck his front legs. He reared. Both pack boxes crashed to the ground beneath his flailing hooves, smashing the plywood, spilling out cans, dishes, oranges . . .

I watched hypnotized as one of his feet landed on a loaf of bread, squishing it paper-thin. At last the big brown gelding stood quivering, sides heaving.

My father clenched his fists. "What's wrong with that horse?"

"The back cinch," I said. "It's in his flanks."

My father stooped to look under the horse's belly. "Yep, there's the problem." As soon as Dad undid the back cinch, Duke relaxed immediately. "Somebody forgot to adjust the keeper," Dad said, frowning. "Michael, you're the one who saddled him. You know you have to check the keeper!"

A keeper is the narrow leather strap that runs under a horse's belly between the front and back cinches to prevent the back cinch from slipping into his flank. Duke's keeper had been left much too long.

Michael bent his head. "I'm sorry."

"Well, I guess I could have checked it, too," my father said.

"Dad, why do you always stick up for him?" I sputtered. "The food, the boxes . . . everything's wrecked. He always messes everything up! Why does he have to be so scatterbrained?"

Michael looked away. "Do you think I like being this way?" he said, his lip quivering.

Dad put his hand on Michael's shoulder. "Never mind. We all need a few faults, don't we?" He turned to Holly. "Those two old beat-up pack boxes in your dad's truck — the ones he keeps all his junk in. We can use them."

We followed Dad to Mr. Wilson's truck and watched him dump out an old bridle, pieces of leather and several brushes.

When we got back to the horses, I asked, "What makes you think Duke is going to let you pack him again?"

Dad laughed. "Of course he will. He just bucked because his cinch was pulled up into his flanks."

"Yeah," I growled, "we'll have to make sure somebody else checks everything this time."

"That's enough!" Dad said, scowling at me.

Holly flipped a smashed orange with the toe of her boot. "Freshly squeezed fruit juice, anyone?" She bent to scoop a handful of broken spaghetti from the ground. "Or would you prefer some nice pasta?"

Michael gulped and tried to smile. "How about mashed potatoes?" he said, kicking at some dirty squashed white things.

"Yuck." Holly grinned. "Maybe it's good this happened. I might be able to lose some weight after all."

Michael looked at her and this time he was really smiling. Then he spread his hands as though trying to circle an enormous object and put on his Shakespeare-quoting voice. "'O! that this too too solid flesh would melt, thaw and resolve itself into a dew . . .'"

Laughing, Holly threw a squashed orange at him. He ducked and it flew over his shoulder.

I grinned, caught by the crazy mood. "Let's hope Michael doesn't lose any weight," I said.

It was like magic. Michael chuckled. "My hollow legs would collapse. I wouldn't be able to stay on my horse."

I laughed too. "We'd have to fill your legs with sand."

"Yeah, it would match the sand in my head," Michael said, his mouth still smiling, but his eyes sad. No, I realized, my brother really didn't like being the way he was.

"Pancake syrup!" Holly picked up an intact plastic bottle, peered at Michael through the top edge of her glasses, and pursed her lips like a little old lady. "Young man, you could live on pancake syrup."

"I'd get too sweet," Michael said.

* * *

While I started organizing what was left of the groceries, Dad sat against a tree, his hands behind his neck. "Good thing the eggs ended up on Ginger," he said.

Holly raised her eyebrows. "Too bad my father can't hear you! Hey, Michael, we should have had a picture of your dad's bucking bronco. Where was your fancy camera when we really needed it?"

"On the truck seat. I think."

We laughed. Michael was always forgetting where he'd left his camera.

Minutes later I had the two boxes balanced perfectly. It was much easier when they weren't full.

Michael carefully buckled the keeper, adjusting it to hold the back cinch just behind Duke's belly, well ahead of his flank.

I watched as Dad tightened Duke's cinches. Yes, the horse did look relaxed and normal again. But when Michael and Dad headed toward him carrying the boxes, Duke's eyes widened, showing white.

"Dad," I called. "He's scared."

My father chuckled. "Of course he's scared. He's just had quite an experience. All that stuff flying around! But as soon as we get him packed again he'll see everything's fine."

Duke quivered and snorted.

I shook my head. "This isn't going to work."

"Dad, maybe Greg is right," said Michael. "Duke sure doesn't look happy."

"Michael, don't you start, too." Dad laughed. "You know he's the best packhorse in the world."

That was the *second* attempt at packing Duke. Half an hour later we were ready for the *third* attempt, and my father certainly wasn't laughing anymore.

Four

Carefully, as though they were handling nitro-glycerin, Dad and Michael lifted the splintered wooden boxes toward Duke's pack saddle. The horse took a step backward, rolling his eyes. "Whoa, boy, easy," said Holly. Duke snorted and hunched his back.

Michael set his box down. "Dad, he isn't going to let us do it. Not now. Maybe never again."

Dad shook his fist at Duke's nose. "Oh, yes, he is!"

Michael gulped and turned away. "It's not bad enough that I lost Patches," he said. "I had to wreck your favorite packhorse . . ." Head bent, he rubbed his hand across his eyes. "Dad, we're going to have to pack Lucky. Greg could ride Duke —"

My eyes widened and I could almost smell smoke coming out of my nostrils. "Me? I'm not riding a bucking bronco. Why not pack Lightning? *You* ride Duke."

Michael's mouth set in a straight hard line. "Lightning has never packed. But Lucky has. And Lightning is too spirited."

"Too spirited? You mean too crazy."

He didn't answer, didn't even look at me.

"So pack Muggs," I said.

"She's never packed, either," Dad answered. "Out here is not the place to train a horse to pack. We can't afford to lose any more groceries. Duke has to do it."

Michael shook his head. "Dad, he's bucked everything off twice now. He won't forget that."

"He'll be all right!" It wasn't very often you heard Dad raise his voice to Michael. You could almost touch the silence as they again lifted the boxes onto Duke's pack saddle. The big horse flattened his ears against his neck, rolling his eyes. Duke, please behave, I thought. Please take the pack. I don't want to ride you.

Holly stroked Duke's neck firmly yet gently, the way you'd rub a sore muscle. "Good boy. Easy does it. Good boy."

Dad's face was white. Michael bit his lip. Together they tied the ropes around the boxes.

And Duke exploded for the third time. But there was something different about it. He seemed to be enjoying himself this time, dancing on the boxes, smashing them with a vengeance, his nostrils flaring, his feet hammering plywood and groceries.

Finally he quit, then stood quietly, surrounded by wood splinters and what had once been food. My father took off his hat, fumbled with it, then turned from us, his shoulders slumped.

I walked after him. "Dad, we'll have to go home.

There's not enough food left. And we don't have any more pack boxes —"

He spun around. "Leave me alone."

Michael touched Dad's arm. Dad's face changed completely as he turned toward Michael. I was left out. There was just the two of them. Michael didn't even glance at me when he spoke. "Dad, let's pack Lucky. Greg can ride Duke."

Dad nodded.

"I am not riding that horse!"

My little brother turned to me and talked slowly as though I were a troublesome child. "Duke is a perfectly behaved saddle horse," he said. "I promise you'll be okay."

"Perfectly behaved? He'll buck me off just like he bucked off the pack boxes."

"No, he won't. You don't even resemble a pack box."

"You think you know everything!" I shouted. "You can't know what a horse is going to do. They're unpredictable. I am not riding that insane creature."

"Then I'll ride him and you can ride Lightning."

"Forget it."

Dad went to the truck and came back with a hammer and some nails. He pulled the broken boxes apart, and from what was left of four pack boxes, started to hammer together two.

"We don't have enough groceries left," I said.

Dad kept hammering. "There's lots of food on Ginger and Smoky," he mumbled. I wondered what it would take to make my father quit.

It was almost one o'clock. The sun burned my back

as I repacked what was left of Duke's load. Within minutes the boxes were balanced and on Lucky.

Holly had Duke saddled for me. The big brown gelding looked at me as though the whole thing had been a joke.

The others mounted, each holding the lead rope of one of the packhorses. "Come on, Greg," Michael said. "Duke won't buck with a rider. Never ever."

By then I was almost wishing Duke *would* throw me, just to show Michael that he didn't know everything, but sure enough when I climbed on, Duke stood quietly. And he walked like a gentleman as we headed down the trail. It's a trick, I thought, my body tense. Any minute he's going to start bucking. He didn't buck the boxes off right away, either.

Clutching the saddle horn, I turned to look once more at Mr. Wilson's beautiful truck and wondered what I'd done to deserve any of this. I felt like waving goodbye as we headed into thick spruce forest and lost sight of the last remnants of civilization.

We came to the river. I'd never crossed a raging river on a horse. In the days before my father had finally conceded that his firstborn son was not going to share his passion for horses, I had taken riding lessons. Obviously mountain trail riding was going to be very different than trotting in circles inside a city arena.

The river was wide and deep and fast, and I knew it would be cold. Icy cold. It wouldn't be much fun if Duke started bucking in the middle of the river.

Dad led the way on Muggs. Everybody always teased Dad about Muggs's big ugly head and Roman nose, but watching Muggs pick her way carefully down the steep muddy bank and into the river, I began to see why he loved her so much. Dad was leading Ginger. With water swirling against their bellies, the two horses moved calmly between huge, almost submerged boulders.

Michael was next. Lightning pranced down the bank and splashed into the river. Michael could ride any horse as though he had been born sitting on its back. He had always been able to. Lucky followed Lightning, not at all bothered by the churning water.

I motioned for Holly. "Ladies first."

"Sure, when the going gets rough." She grinned and pushed up her glasses with the same hand that was holding Smoky's lead rope. Down the bank Bud pranced and twisted. Holly could sure ride. This was her first mountain trail ride, yet she seemed so confident. I knew she had ridden all her life, but I still expected her to be a bit uneasy in unfamiliar terrain.

In the middle of the river, Bud tripped and nearly fell, but Holly rode him easily while he fought to gain his balance. Smoky followed sedately as Bud plunged through the water and leapt up the muddy bank.

Neither Michael nor Dad had stopped to be sure that we had crossed safely. That made me mad. They knew full well that Holly and I had never ridden across a river before. I knew it wasn't that they didn't care what happened to us. It was just that they had done it so often they couldn't even imagine anybody being scared. Still, it made me mad. Holly turned her head to check on me, but then Bud swerved, and she had to concentrate on him.

It was my turn. Duke, please don't buck now. Not in the river. Please.

The big horse pushed his legs against the current, placing his hooves carefully among the uneven rocks of the river bottom.

The water blurred past. To look down at it made me instantly dizzy. Not good. Forcing my eyes up, focusing on the willows at the other side, I tried to steer Duke directly across the river, but then we started drifting downstream fast. So I tried angling him toward a spot far upstream and was pleased to find that we then headed straight across.

Duke was behaving perfectly, moving carefully against the powerful river. How could this possibly be the same horse that had just bucked off our pack boxes three times? And why did Michael always have to be right?

When Duke climbed out of the river, I realized my boots were soaking wet. I hadn't thought to lift my feet.

We rode through thick spruce up a hillside. Duke still hadn't bucked. His head nodded in rhythm to the thud of his footsteps along the dirt trail. Michael turned around and smiled. "Pretty good saddle horse, eh?"

I made a face. "Yeah, I guess you're not as dumb as you look." He hated it when I said that. But I couldn't let him get too conceited.

We headed down the hill and I could hear the roar of water again. "How many rivers do we have to cross?" I yelled.

Dad turned around to answer. "All the same river. Fox River. The trail crosses it about eight times before we reach Forbidden Valley."

"Fun and games," I muttered.

Dad headed Muggs into the river, and we all splashed in behind him. I lifted my boots high this time, but they still ended up getting soaked.

It was at the fourth crossing, just when I'd begun to think this was no big thing, that we ran into trouble.

The channel ran narrow and deeper, and the boulders were bigger. In the middle of the river, Bud decided to spin around. Smoky's lead rope slipped under Bud's tail. And Bud went crazy.

Right there in shoulder-deep water, he reared. A horse standing on two legs in a raging river couldn't be stable. He toppled. Michael and Dad had already vanished into the thick willows on the other side.

I saw Holly's white face hit the water. "Dad! Michael!" I yelled. Bud's head slid into the churning river. Then the current carried Bud away with Holly half under him, tangled in Smoky's lead rope.

Five

"Holly!" I stared at the place where she had disappeared, then scanned the swirling water for a sign, any sign, of her. Farther downstream, Bud struggled to climb the bank, his hooves clattering against the rocks. Somehow Smoky had escaped from the tangle and stood across the river, water pouring from his lopsided pack. But where was Holly?

Finally she appeared, a blur of hands grabbing frantically at a boulder, slipping, falling back, pulled farther and farther downstream. I sat helpless and frozen on Duke, still in the middle of the roaring river. What good would it do if I jumped in?

I didn't even have a rope. Dad and Michael both had nice long lariats tied to their saddles, neatly coiled, ready for any emergency. But neither of them had had the common sense to wait to be sure we had crossed the river successfully.

"Dad! Michael!" My voice sounded squeaky.

Then Holly disappeared. Just when I thought she was a goner, there she was, hanging onto a boulder farther along the bank. She clung to the rock, one arm back and around it, struggling against the current, desperately trying to pull herself up onto it. I kicked Duke. He leapt through the river and up the other side, then I turned him toward Holly and kicked him harder. She was still hanging on.

Trying to trot on the rocks, Duke lost his footing and almost went down. I reined him to a walk, riding as close as possible, then jumped off and scrambled over the stones, stumbling and tripping. "Hang on, Holly!" I shouted.

She seemed to slip down, back into the swirling water as I reached the big rock. I grabbed her shoulders and pulled, amazed at how much strength I found in my shaking arms.

As I pulled, Holly heaved and pushed, trying to help me. When I managed to get her up onto the boulder, she collapsed, coughing, gasping for breath, shivering violently. She needed to be covered. I ran to Duke, untied my jacket from behind the saddle, fingers fumbling, clumsy, as though I were wearing mitts, then stumbled back over the rocks to kneel beside Holly.

She didn't seem to have any injuries, no cuts, no broken bones. I wrapped my jacket around her wet shaking shoulders, barely aware that my own muscles had started to tremble from shock.

Something was very different about her. I forced my brain to think. What was it? Something bad. And then it hit me. Her glasses. She had lost her glasses. She would be totally helpless without them.

The stones along the bank rattled, and I turned to see Michael and Dad riding toward us.

I lost control. "Nice of you to check on us now!"

They jumped off their horses, mumbling they were sorry. My hands now shook with anger. "Oh, thanks. Apologies help a lot. And she's lost her glasses."

Holly spoke for the first time. "Greg, it's okay —"

"What do you mean, okay?" I blurted. "You'll be blind. You won't even be able to see to get on your bloody horse!"

"I have another pair. In my duffel bag."

Michael laughed. It was probably just nervous laughter from the tension, but it sure struck me the wrong way. I jumped up and attacked him, pounding with my fists. He fell backward onto the rocks and lay curled with his arms around his head, cowering from me. For some reason that made me even angrier. "Get up, you wimp!"

But when he lifted his head, my stomach lurched at the sight of blood spurting from his nose. He wiped at it with the back of his hand, smearing red across his face, staring at me out of wide terrified eyes.

"Greg!" Dad grabbed my arms, but he didn't need to. Seeing the blood had drained the fight from me. In its place had come a cold feeling of dread. What if my brother had hit his head when he fell on those rocks? Just thinking of it made me hate him even more, in a frightening kind of way. Dad and Michael had caused all this by not watching us cross the river, and I was the one who had to end up in so much trouble, looking so bad.

I could feel Dad trembling as I hung limp against his

arms. He let me go, breathing hard as though he'd been running. "Greg, don't you dare do anything like that again," he gasped.

Michael was sitting crouched, blood pouring from his nose. The tight feeling pushed itself higher, choking my throat. "Pinch off your nose," I said.

Michael obeyed instantly, and my emotions churned. I felt guilty, ashamed, angry, frightened. Stumbling to the river, I bent to scoop water onto my face. Its iciness soothed some of the pain inside my chest.

Bud was moving toward us, his reins dragging. A couple of times he stepped on them and his head jerked up, his eyes rolling white. His drenched sides were heaving.

Kneeling on the rocks beside Michael, Dad glared at me and opened his mouth as though he were going to shout something, but he didn't say a word. Then he turned to Holly. Her whole body was shaking. "Holly, you have to get some dry clothes on," Dad said. His lips tightened as he looked back at me. "Can you remember which packhorse is carrying Holly's duffel?"

"Ginger." My eyes avoided Dad's.

Dad started to unpack Ginger. Michael stood up to help, still pinching off his nose with a blood-smeared hand. They removed the tarp and Dad handed Holly her duffel bag. She stood up, shivering, and smiled weakly. The first thing she did was rummage through her bag, squinting, her nose almost in it. Was she ever near-sighted! Finally she pulled out a small red velvet case, opened it and put on the glasses. "My old pair." She wrinkled her face and grinned. "They make me look even uglier than normal."

"You're not ugly," Dad said.

She laughed. "It was almost worth getting dunked just to hear that."

"Good you brought a second pair," I mumbled.

"I always do. Everywhere." Water was dripping from her hair onto her glasses. Shivering, she fished around in her duffel bag, found a towel, wiped the lenses and put them back on. Then she wrapped the towel around her head.

"Holly, you'd better change your clothes right now," Dad said, "or you'll get pneumonia. Look how you're shaking."

Holly glanced at the river. "Yeah, somebody forgot to turn up the heat in that swimming pool."

We laughed. All of us.

After she disappeared behind some bushes to change her clothes, Dad and Michael lifted Holly's duffel bag onto Ginger again and tied down the tarp. My eyes kept drifting to Michael's face, to the smeared blood. His lip was beginning to swell. I could still feel the impact of my knuckles against his face and could see him fall backward onto those rocks. I felt shaky just thinking about it.

Holly returned, holding her wet clothes. "I tried to wring them out . . ."

"We'll tie them on top of the pack," Dad said. "The sun dries things better than any electric clothes dryer."

The hot sunshine felt really good to me. It must have felt wonderful on Holly's freezing skin.

At the next river crossing, both Dad and Michael stopped on the other side, watching to be sure we all made it through safely. By then Michael's face was so puffy that I cringed every time he turned around. It was the first time I'd ever hit him like that. When we were little kids we had punched each other, but never anything like this. The knot in my stomach wouldn't go away.

We rode through brush, along hillsides, through thick spruce forest, crossed the river another two or three times, and passed a couple of empty campsites. Funny thing, in Calgary we could see a ridge of mountains all along the western horizon. Here we were almost two hundred kilometers northwest of Calgary, riding right into the mountains, but we couldn't really see anything because of the thick forest enclosing us.

Suddenly the horses stopped and snorted. Two deer jumped across the trail in front of us, bouncing as though on springs.

A few minutes later we crossed a muddy creek, then rode through willows so tall and close that they slapped our faces. As the trail headed back into the forest, we met a man on a gray horse, leading three packhorses tied head to tail. Dad asked, "Have you seen a stray pinto anywhere?"

"Nope." The man stopped his horses, staring at Michael's face.

"We lost a horse last week," Dad said.

"Too bad," said the guy. "Could be anywhere by now. Good luck."

We rode on. No one spoke a word. I was getting hungry, but there was no use asking if we could stop and unpack something to eat.

A cold wind began to blow and the sky clouded over.

Within a few minutes it started to rain lightly. We were riding along a ledge with no trees to shelter us from the sharpness of the wind. I watched Michael turn to untie his jacket and yellow rain slicker from behind the saddle, holding Lightning's reins with Lucky's halter rope in his left hand.

While he was putting on the big rubberized raincoat, it billowed in the wind like a sail. Lightning jumped and pranced, but Michael handled him easily. Dad had absolutely no problem putting on his jacket and slicker. It seemed as though nothing could make Muggs misbehave.

With one hand I untied the jacket and rain slicker from the back of my saddle. What would Duke do when I tried to put the slicker on? What if he thought it was a pack tarp and started bucking? But Duke just kept walking even when the wind slapped the slicker against his flanks.

I looked down at my hands. They were covered with grime from Duke's neck and the reins.

Light rain soon changed to a downpour. Holly was trying to untie her slicker, her face worried.

"Let's stop, Dad," Michael called. "Bud might go crazy when Holly tries to put her slicker on."

Michael dismounted and held the four horses. And sure enough, as the wind caught Holly's raincoat, Bud reared, snorting, eyes wide. "'Rough winds do shake the darling buds of May,'" said Michael.

I groaned. Shakespeare at a time like this. But Holly laughed. "Buds! Michael, that was a good one!" She looked at Bud, laughing again. "'Rough winds *do* shake the darling Bud of May! Only trouble is, this is July."

"Feels cold enough to be May," Michael replied, a lopsided grin on his puffy face.

"True!" Holly shivered. "I bet the temperature's dropped ten degrees in the last few minutes. What happened to our nice warm sunny day?"

"That's the mountains for you," Dad said. "Out here the weather changes in the blink of an eye. We say, 'If you don't like the weather, just wait a minute.'"

"Sure," Michael snorted. "Wait a minute, because it will probably get worse."

"Hey, what about Holly's clothes!" I said. They were still tied to the top of Smoky's pack and the rain was soaking them.

Holly laughed. "This must be the rinse cycle."

Even with Michael holding Bud, Holly had difficulty climbing on again with her slicker flopping around her legs. Bud reared a couple of times before he finally gave in. "I hope we find Patches pretty soon," she muttered.

The wind became even sharper. What a relief when the trail wound again into forest. But the rain continued to pour. We rode on, silent yellow-clad figures in the gray afternoon, and I shuddered at the thought of riding through cold clammy rain, day after day.

The trail was becoming muddy. The horses slipped as they went down a steep hill. Then as abruptly as it had started, the rain stopped. Within minutes the wind had blown all the clouds to the east, leaving blue sky and warm golden sunshine. "I don't believe it," Holly said. "We just got our raincoats on."

We took the slickers off and tied them behind the saddles again. Holly managed to control Bud amazingly well. He only reared once as she gently moved her arm out of her sleeve.

The narrow trail gave way to a wide grassy corridor with forest on either side. Duke started to pass the other horses, his ears flattened. When he reached the front of the line, he pointed his ears forward and walked even faster over the wet grass. I turned around and asked Dad, "What's his hurry?"

"Duke loves to lead," Dad answered. "When the trail opens up like this, he always wants to pass."

It felt strange to be in the front of the line, a feeling of control and yet vulnerability, especially with everybody's eyes on my back. Ever since I had hit Michael, they had all been acting pretty cold toward me.

When the trail headed back into the forest, I felt a tinge of fear. You never knew what was around a corner. I thought of bears and wondered what would happen if we met one. I was glad that Dad had his rifle along, resting within easy reach in the scabbard tied to his saddle.

Six

The trail climbed again, much steeper this time. Suddenly rain started to pelt down as though someone had turned on a fire hose. By the time we put our slickers on again, it had stopped raining. Within a few more minutes the sky had cleared once more and the sun was scorching us.

"This weather really is crazy," Holly said.

Michael pulled his swollen lips into a grin. "'So foul and fair a day I have not seen.'" More Shakespeare. This guy was driving me insane. If only we could find Holly's stupid horse tonight and head back tomorrow morning.

When the trail leveled out into a huge meadow, the sun seemed even hotter. My head sweated under the heavy soggy cowboy hat with its tight restrictive band. No wonder everybody always had greasy hair when they'd been trail riding a few days. I took the hat off and hung it over my saddle horn, but then the sun burned my eyes.

At last the trail climbed into more thick shady forest. The horses were puffing. My rear end hurt more and more. Saddles should have pillows built into them. Big thick pillows.

Just when I was beginning to wonder when we'd ever get there, we rode out of the trees and below us saw a vast green valley stretching to the horizon, with a river running through it, and snow-capped mountains surrounding its forested hillsides. "Forbidden Valley," Dad said.

"Wow." Holly's eyes were sparkling behind her funny old glasses. "That's pretty enough for a postcard."

"Oh, no!" Michael slapped a hand to his forehead. "I forgot my camera back in the truck."

"I put it in my saddlebag." Dad grinned. "You'd lose your head if it weren't so firmly attached."

We rode down the hill to a large campsite. I slid off Duke, groaning, unable to believe how sore and stiff I felt. My knees didn't want to straighten.

Driving around in a car obviously didn't keep a person in shape. I hadn't ridden a horse for years, and my whole body was objecting to the ordeal.

Holly swung easily off her saddle. "So this is where you think we'll find old Patches?"

"Yep," Dad said. "He's probably hanging around somebody's horses somewhere in this valley." He tied Muggs to a tree and gave her a couple of pats on the neck. "A horse wouldn't stay by himself way up at Sky Lake this long. He'd wander back down here, back the way he came in."

Holly nodded. "Patches always likes to head for home and he hates to be alone."

Dad pointed to one of the mountains. "Sky Lake is up there. Just a bit in front of that pass. You can't see the lake until you're right there. The trail continues past the lake down to another staging area called Cutbank Creek, about twenty-five kilometers north of where we parked our trucks. Lots of people ride into Sky Lake from there. The north trail is an easier way into the lake."

Michael had to get involved, too. "Easier but not nearly as spectacular!" He pointed to the right of the pass. "The trail from here to the lake goes just below that high ridge, but you can ride way up there, right along the ridge instead. Talk about a view. You'd love it, Holly."

My body was crying with pain. The last thing I felt like was listening to Dad and Michael give a geography lesson. I sighed and headed for a stump. But no, sitting down didn't seem like a good idea.

Finally the geography lesson was over. It seemed to take forever to unpack and unsaddle the horses and then set up camp. Luckily there were A-frame poles, a ridgepole and some firewood left in this camp just as there had been in most of the other camps we'd passed. The idea of chopping wood to cook supper made my aching body cringe. Just helping to put the tent up proved to be a major effort, even though the others did more than their share. None of them seemed stiff at all.

We led the horses to the meadow. While we were buckling leather and chain hobbles like handcuffs above their front hooves, the animals started tearing at the grass as though they hadn't eaten for days. I watched them graze, their hobbles forcing them to take tiny mincing steps. They were trapped out here and so was I. The only difference was that they didn't seem to mind.

Waddling back to camp, I wondered how I was going to survive riding from morning to night, day after day. Three hours in the saddle had already crippled me. Michael, Holly and my forty-six-year-old Dad weren't suffering at all.

Not suffering from riding, anyway. Obviously Michael's lip was hurting him. It had swollen badly, and so had his eye. It wasn't usual for him to be so quiet. He hadn't even complained yet about being hungry.

Dad brought up the subject of food. "Guess we'd better cook supper before Michael fades out on us." He chopped wood into kindling and built a fire, dirt sticking to the spruce sap coating his hands. Then he rummaged through the boxes looking for the frying pan and hamburger meat, smudging everything greasy black. "Good," he said when he finally found the meat. "It's almost thawed out."

Dad, Michael and Holly dug around in the boxes, scattering things all over the place, looking for the carrots and onions. Then they had to search for the salt and pepper. When they had finally stuffed everything back in the boxes, Dad said, "Oh, we forgot the spaghetti."

I didn't offer to help, but didn't make any comment, either. They were still all acting less than friendly toward me, and Michael's face looked awful.

Instead I found a bar of soap and trudged down to the river. Over and over I lathered my hands in the ice-cold water, trying to get them clean, then made my way back to camp.

No one talked much to me while supper was cooking over the smoky fire. Dad and Michael lashed two thick boughs between a couple of trees and laid four of the pack boxes on them horizontally, like shelves of a cupboard.

"That's smart," I said. "Where did you guys learn to do that?"

"Everybody does it," Dad said. "That's the way you set up a camp kitchen so you can organize things better." But it didn't seem to help much. When supper was ready, they still had to search for the dishes and the cutlery. "It's sure hard to find anything in these boxes," Holly said.

Dad laughed. "When we're trail riding we always spend half our time searching through pack boxes."

After supper, they rummaged around for the detergent, dishcloth and pot scraper. Dad said, "I'd better go find a dead tree to chop down so we'll have enough firewood to cook breakfast. I guess I can trust you three to do the dishes without any major incidents." I didn't like the way he looked at me when he said that, even though I knew he was trying to be funny.

"I'll wash the dishes," Holly said. "Best way for a person to get clean hands around here."

Michael grabbed the dish towel. "What if I put the dishes away?" I said. "And while I'm at it, I'll organize the cupboards so it'll be easier to find things."

No one objected. "Dishes and cutlery go in this cupboard, all the cooking supplies in that one . . ." I muttered as I went ahead. "Cans over there . . . bread in one of those closed boxes on the ground . . ." How much food would be left when we headed home?

Maybe we'd find Holly's horse the next morning and I'd be repacking and balancing this pile of stuff all over again.

I stood up to stretch my aching back. Holly was washing the last few plates. Grease and food particles floated on the rinse water. Holly's hands were indeed clean, pink and almost raw-looking. But as soon as she started washing the fire-blackened pots and pans, those clean wrinkly hands were once again coated with greasy soot.

When she poured out the dishwater, Holly asked if I wanted any help.

I shook my head. "It's easier for one person. Thanks anyway."

She smiled. "Lucky you said no. Organizing things isn't one of my talents. Good somebody can do it, though."

Michael sat down on a block of wood, his head resting on his hands, his elbows on his knees. Normally he'd be reading a book or be out in the meadow talking to Lightning.

His bruised face made me flinch. I knew he was in a lot of pain, but he hadn't said a word about it. That made me feel worse. Michael was so quiet that I found myself missing his usual chatter.

It felt good to be doing something where I could be in control again. And this organizing would help everyone. They'd all be able to find things much more easily. When I had everything sorted, I arranged taller things toward the back of the boxes and shorter things at the front so you could see everything with no trouble at all.

While I worked on the boxes, Dad was busy sawing

firewood and chopping kindling. Dad could split a piece of wood with one powerful deft stroke. It looked so easy when he did it, but it was a skill that took hours of practice. Michael and Holly brought the horses in and tied them to trees for the night.

When I finished with the pack-box cupboards, Dad said, "That looks real good, Greg."

Michael's puffy mouth curved upward. "Yeah, even I should be able to find things now."

"Uh, thanks," I said, glad that at least they seemed to appreciate something I had done. Sitting on a stump, shifting my sore bottom, I wondered how to spend the rest of the evening. No TV to watch. No radio. It was too early to go to bed. Maybe a walk might help relax my stiff sore body.

I set out along the edge of the meadow. The sky was almost dark, but there was enough of a moon to light my way. In the distance a coyote howled. I stopped to listen. Another one answered, quite a bit closer. The sound floated, mournful and eerie in the cool mountain air.

More coyotes joined in the chorus. I'd never heard coyotes howl before, except in movies. The hair stood up on my arms, and I shivered. Then an unfamiliar feeling of peace spread over my body as though my muscles were melting. Only five more days until Amanda's party. Yet, out here it seemed strange even to imagine such things as loud music, dancing, pulsating lights . . .

I walked for a long time, glad that Dad had insisted we all wear hiking boots instead of cowboy boots. "You never know how far you might need to walk," he had told us.

I came to a fallen tree and sat on it, motionless, my nostrils filling with the smell of spruce. Then, reluctantly, I headed back to camp.

I could hear their voices, first muffled, gradually a few more words, clearer and louder. "It has to be there somewhere." That was Dad talking. "Maybe in the box on the ground. Over there."

Michael seemed to mumble, but soon I was close enough to hear what he was saying. "We can't go to bed without cocoa."

I hurried into camp. And in the firelight I could see them. Holly was sitting on a stump reading a book with her little flashlight. Dad was brushing his teeth at the riverbank. And Michael? Michael was rummaging around in the boxes.

Everything was scattered all over. All my work. Gone. It looked as though a bear had been in camp. Groceries on top of the cupboards, on the ground, everywhere. The peaceful feeling disappeared and something exploded deep inside me.

Seven

"**W**hat do you think you're doing?" I bellowed. Michael twisted around, his eyes frightened. "I can't find the cocoa."

"Get out of those boxes."

"I was going to put everything back."

"Get out of those boxes."

"But . . ."

Please, God, don't let me hit him again. His face, swollen and tight, glowed in the yellow light of the fire. I willed my fists to stay by my sides, then spun away into the darkness.

Minutes later, I plunked myself down on the grassy riverbank. It felt damp, cold and very hard under my sore bottom. Oh, for a soft upholstered chair. Oh, to be back home.

A flashlight beam moved in my direction. "Greg? Greg?" It was Holly. Best to be quiet. Maybe she wouldn't find me.

But the beam swung and came straight for where I was sitting. "Greg?"

"What do you want?"

She didn't answer, just sat beside me on the cold riverbank, then turned off her flashlight. I plucked a blade of grass and put it in my mouth, turning my back to her. For a couple of minutes we sat in silence.

Then she spoke softly. "Greg, I was the one who suggested the cocoa. And Michael offered to make some for all of us. But he was going to put everything back in order."

I laughed. "Oh, sure he was!"

Her voice strengthened. "Why do you always think the worst about Michael? While he was looking for the cocoa, he kept saying how he hated to mess up all your work. He just moved everything out to search —"

"You should see his room at home."

"So what? Why should it bother you if *his* room is messy?"

"He's a slob. And Dad's just like him," I said. "Maybe not quite so bad." I shouldn't be telling Holly things like that, washing our dirty linen in public, as my grandma would say, but I couldn't seem to stop myself.

"Greg, why does it matter so much to you?" she asked, her voice softening again.

"Because when I was little Mom was always pleading with Dad, begging him to pick up his clothes, keep his desk tidy, pick up the garden tools . . ."

Once I had started talking it seemed like I couldn't quit. I told her how Mom had always joked that it might be too late to work on my dad, but she was going to teach her two sons to be neat even if it killed her. I didn't mention how my mother used to laugh when she said that, laugh with a funny catch in her voice that had twisted my insides.

"Maybe Mom ran out of energy, working so hard to program neatness into me," I said, trying to smile, "because she never did manage to program Michael."

Holly wrapped her arms around her knees. "Your mom and you are sure alike," she said gently. "You both need things to be just so in your lives. Maybe that's why your mom loves being an accountant and you're crazy about math. Because math is pure. When an answer is right, it's right, all under control, no messy edges."

"It feels scary when things are out of control," I said, then swallowed hard. "Like sometimes between Michael and me . . ."

I'd never talked like this to any other girl. It was ironic, though, because that was one of my best lines, to tell each and every girl that I'd never been able to talk to anyone else like I could talk to her. Girls always fell for it.

Trouble was, it was true now, but I didn't dare say it to this very different girl. Thick, yes. Thick waist, thick bones, thick glasses. But definitely not thick in the head.

"By the way," she said, "thanks for pulling me out of the river."

"My privilege." I leaned back. Most of the anger had slipped away. I put my hands behind my head and looked up to a half moon and thousands of stars. "I've never seen so many stars before."

"Me neither," she said, staring at the sky. "You can hardly see any stars in the city. The lights drown most of them out. That's awful, isn't it?"

Some of the stars were huge and very bright. Hundreds of others were just pinpricks that together made clusters of white haze.

We sat without speaking for a while then. The only noise was the gurgling of the river and the occasional cry of a coyote or the hoot of an owl. Strange to feel so relaxed around a girl, as though we were friends, and I didn't need to impress her, because she could see through me and understand.

Then she wrecked the whole mood. "Greg, I just hate it that you and Michael are always fighting. Because there's nothing in this whole world I'd rather have than a brother or a sister."

"Well, too bad." I turned from her.

"Why do you let him upset you so easily?"

"Because he's absentminded and messy, and he never thinks about the results of what he says or does, and he talks too much."

"So? Like your dad said, everybody needs some faults. Anyway, different people have different ideas of what's a fault and what isn't. Maybe he thinks you're too tense and too judgmental."

"Why are you sticking up for him?"

"I'm not. I'm sticking up for both of you."

"Well, you sure have a funny way of doing it." I jumped to my feet and strode back to camp.

Dad was staring into the fire. "Hi," he said.

I forced a smile. "Hi."

Then I noticed that everything had been put back into

the pack-box cupboards, all in order of height, all in groups just the way I'd organized them. I glanced at Dad. He said only, "Michael." Then he stared into the fire again.

Michael was already asleep when I went into the tent. I stood for a moment watching him. Light from the camp fire shone through the canvas walls, giving his face an eerie yellow glow. With his swollen lips moving in and out as he snored, he looked downright ugly. Yet he seemed helpless, like a very young child, with his soft brown hair rumpled and messy over the edge of the sleeping bag.

When we were little kids, Michael and I had been able to play together happily — at least sometimes. Why did I react so violently to him now? He was my brother. We should still be able to be friends.

When Holly came into the tent I pretended to be asleep. She crawled into her sleeping bag. A little while later Dad came to bed. The night filled with noises — horses munching and shuffling, coyotes crying, an owl hooting. I expected to be awake for a long time because of my saddle-sore body and churning feelings, but I soon dozed off.

* * *

The acrid smell of smoke nudged through my sleep. Terrified, I sat up, then realized where I was. Someone had made a fire to cook breakfast. I looked at my watch. Almost eight o'clock.

As soon as I emerged from the tent I noticed that everything was still organized in the pack boxes even though all three people were busy making breakfast.

That should have made me feel good. I mean, if I'd won, why did I feel so guilty and uncomfortable?

"Morning, Greg," Dad said, flipping pancakes with one hand, holding the frying pan with the other and trying to use his shoulders to rub smoke out of his red eyes. "This wood doesn't want to burn." He laughed. "Hope you don't mind your pancakes smoked and half-raw." How could he be enjoying himself so much?

The horses were out grazing. Freshly sawn logs and some chopped kindling were piled against a tree.

"How many pancakes can you eat?" Dad asked me. "Two."

"Just two? If you go this easy on the grub, you might foil Duke's efforts to starve Michael. That old horse didn't dance all over our groceries for nothing, you know."

Michael laughed, but it was a strained kind of laugh. And his face looked worse than before.

Dad flipped the pancakes onto my plate. "Greg, you don't have to ride Duke today," he said. "We'll be leaving the extra horses in camp. So you can ride Lucky."

"Aw, Duke's okay," I said. "No use breaking in another bronco," I added when I noticed his eyebrows arch in surprise.

The plan was to spend the day visiting camps farther down the valley to find out if anybody had seen Patches. Maybe he had followed some trail riders and might still be hanging around their horses.

I looked toward the meadow. "Hey, Lightning isn't hobbled."

Dad chuckled. "Michael has made such a pet out of

that horse that he'd never run away. Sometimes he sticks too close to camp. You'll see."

Sure enough, while we were doing dishes, Lightning strolled in for a visit. Michael reached into his pocket for a handful of oats. The horse chewed the grain, then pushed his head against Michael's hip to ask for more.

Michael draped his arm over Lightning's neck, leaning his face against the horse's head. Strange how Lightning could be so gentle when Michael wasn't on him and so spirited when he was. But that was the way my brother liked his horse.

Michael still wasn't saying much, but after we started riding, he seemed to relax and began to talk again, first to Dad and then to Holly.

"Sure nice not to have to lead packhorses all the time," he said to her. "But it is kind of dangerous to leave them in camp. Wild horses might bother them while we're gone. We know a guy who left some horses tied in camp, and when he returned that night he was wondering why the ground was so churned up around one of the mares, but he figured she must just have been trying to get loose."

He paused for effect. "Guess what. Eleven months later the guy found a brand-new foal in the pasture with his horses. Turned out it was that mare's foal. From the time he'd left the mare back in camp."

Holly looked skeptical. Dad grinned. "It's true. You can't believe everything Michael tells you, but I'll verify that story."

We passed a well-used trail that led across the river and then up a hill into the forest. "That's the trail to Sky Lake," Michael said to Holly. "I sure wish there was some way you could get to see the lake while we're here."

By the time we reached the first camp site, Michael was his usual talkative self. As we approached the tent, a short guy sauntered out to meet us.

Dad started to chat with the man about the weather. Holly couldn't wait. "Excuse me, sir. Have you seen a pinto? Brown and white. He's kind of fat and sway-backed. He's my horse and he got away last week."

The man looked thoughtful, then his eyes lit up. "Yeah, come to think of it, I seen a fat swaybacked pinto in the next camp up the valley. When we was riding yesterday evening. He was with their horses, grazing. Could be theirs. Could be yours too, I guess."

Holly leaned forward in her saddle. "Did he have a white mark on his forehead like a number seven?"

"Miss, I just seen him from far away. I didn't have my telescope along."

The guy invited us in for coffee, but we declined, anxious to move on.

The man had been staring at Michael. Finally he asked it. "What happened to your face, son? Looks like you ran into a bit of a fight."

Dad and Holly sat as though paralyzed. Michael gulped, then looked away toward the hills, completely avoiding my eyes. "I fell on some rocks by the river."

"Funny kind of fall to give you a shiner like that."

Dad cleared his throat. "Well, we'd better be on our way."

When we rode on, Holly said, "Do you think it really could be Patches?"

Michael answered, "Sure. They'll have him there

tied with their horses." He smiled and the life came back into his eyes. "They'll be wondering what to do with such a beautiful creature."

Holly chuckled. "How would they have caught him?"

Michael was enjoying himself now. "They put oats in a bear trap."

I almost dared to hope, too. We could be on our way back to Calgary by tomorrow morning. Heavy rhythmic party music could help a person forget things. I looked down at my dirt-coated hands and carefully shifted my rear end in the saddle. By tomorrow all of this might seem like just a crazy dream.

But when we arrived at the next camp it was empty. Completely empty.

Eight

"Gone," I said. "Now what? They must have just left."

Michael jumped off his horse and put his hand down to feel the camp-fire ashes. Why couldn't I have thought of that?

"Absolutely cold," he said. "And there's no fresh manure under the trees. This can't be the camp the guy was talking about. I'll bet there's another one just ahead and it won't be empty."

We rode for a few more minutes and saw horses grazing near some big tents. Michael smiled.

"You're not as dumb as you look," I said, then wished I hadn't. Michael hadn't told the guy about my hitting him. For once I owed him something good.

Duke whinnied to the horses, his whole body vibrating beneath me as he called. Several whinnied back.

Then I saw the pinto. Just over the edge of the slope by the trees. A fat swaybacked pinto. Michael pointed. "Holly . . ."

But she had already seen him. Standing in her stir-rups, she leaned forward, peering with her hand over her eyes. The anticipation faded from her face. She sat back into the saddle and said, "It's not him."

"How can you tell from this far away?" I asked.

"I just know."

We rode into camp. A couple of women, a kid and three men were fishing by the creek. Four cowboys were saddling horses. Obviously they were outfitting for paid guests. By now we were close enough to the pinto to confirm that he wasn't Patches. No white number-seven mark on his forehead, and his other markings were different too.

We stopped to talk to the outfitters. They hadn't seen a stray pinto gelding anywhere. They were taking their guests up to Sky Lake for the day. "You ever been up there?" asked one of the guys.

Dad nodded. "It's one of my favorite places. Actually that's where we lost our horse. We were up there Wednesday —"

"You weren't at Sky Lake Friday afternoon?"

"No, we looked all over for him up there and decided he must have come down here. So Friday morning we headed down too."

"You were lucky. Because that afternoon we got caught in a terrible blizzard up there."

"Blizzard?" Holly asked. "A blizzard in July?"

"It just rained at this level," Michael said. How come he had to answer? The guys were staring at Michael's bruised face, but at least they had the decency not to comment on it.

"Hope the weather stays good today," said another

guy as he bridled a horse. "You can sure get freak snowstorms up high. On Friday when the mountain clouded over up there, I wanted to head back right away. But our dudes were all excited about catching fish and said they were too saddle sore to head back without a few hours' rest in the warm sunshine by the lake."

"Yeah," said the other man, "by the time we were halfway down the mountain, them horses were knee-deep in heavy wet snow."

Dad shook his head. "But when the weather's good up there, it's pure heaven. I'm hoping we find our horse pretty soon so we have time to take a day's ride up to Sky Lake. Or maybe we'll even have time to camp up there a couple of days before we have to head back. I'd like Greg and Holly to see it."

Holly's eyes lit up. "That would be great!"

With horror I realized we might be stuck out here for the whole week whether or not we found Patches. I felt betrayed, tricked.

"Yeah, you should take them up there." The man flung a saddle on the next horse. "It'd be a pity for anyone to come all the way out here and not see some really high country. Our dudes grumble and groan all the way up, but they love Sky Lake once they get there."

"And, Dad," said Michael, excited, "on the way, we could take Holly and Greg along the top of the ridge where it's like you can see the whole world!" I wanted to choke him in front of everybody.

"We don't usually take our dudes along that ridge. Kinda dangerous. But it is mighty pretty, I'll say that.

Sure does seem like you see the whole world from up there."

We talked a bit more, but could tell that they wanted to get on with their work. The minute we rode out of the camp I tackled Dad about this new development. "Just in case you don't happen to remember, I'd like to help get things ready for that party. If we find Holly's stupid horse, we're not wasting any more time riding up a mountain just to see some lake and a view."

"You might like it," Michael said quietly. "And it's only a couple of hours from our camp."

I scowled at him, then turned back to Dad. "Look, the deal was we search for the horse, find it and head back to Calgary. This is not my idea of a good time, you know."

"I'd love to see some high country," said Holly.

I felt ready to explode. "You mean I'm trapped either way? If we hurry up and find your stupid horse —"

"Quit calling him stupid." She glared at me.

"Oh, sorry." I lowered my voice. "If we hurry up and find your intelligent horse, then we'll have the privilege of riding all over the mountains for the rest of the week. Won't that be fun?"

Dad answered. "As long as we get you back for your party, we've kept our side of the bargain." That made me fume even more.

We rode farther up the valley, but the other camps were empty. At noon we stopped beside a creek for lunch.

Dad opened a can of salmon. On a leg of his dirty jeans, he laid a slice of bread, then reached for the plastic container that held the butter. The butter was liquid from the heat of the sun and from hours in the saddlebag over the horse's warm flank. Dad dribbled the yellow liquid over his bread, then spooned on some salmon, not even noticing the piece of grass and dirt floating on the surface of the can of fish.

Everyone's hands were black. "Don't worry." Dad laughed as though he could read my thoughts. "A little dirt is good for you." This was more than a little dirt. This was a thick layer of grime and soot mixed with the sticky spruce pitch that coated our hands every time we handled firewood or even tied a horse to a tree.

I forced my stiff legs to bend so I could wash some of the dirt off in the stream. Remember to put a bar of soap in your pocket next time, I told myself. My hands turned red and clumsy in the frigid water. "How can water be this cold in July?" I muttered.

Of course Michael had to answer. "Glaciers. It's from melting glaciers."

"Wow, you're not as dumb as you look," I said, wiping my hands on my jacket. He turned from me, scowling.

The others were already eating. I held a slice of bread on my palm and started to make a sandwich. The melted butter soaked into the bread. I spread a thick layer of salmon over it, took a bite and was surprised at how good it tasted.

Michael pointed to the ground beside him. "Hey, rock jasmines!" Why would he be excited about a bunch of tiny plain white flowers? They looked like weeds to me, hundreds of them in a patch around a big rock.

"Their Latin name is *An-dro-sa-ce cham-ae-jas-me*,"

Michael said. I groaned but everybody ignored me. The name had rolled off Michael's tongue like a chant.

My brother had always loved the sound of big words, even when he was little. Maybe that was why he was so loony about Shakespeare. When he was in grade one, Michael had learned the names of all the dinosaurs and had driven me crazy reciting them at the table.

"Rock jasmine?" Holly smiled. "Say its botanical name again."

Michael said it slower this time, with even more rhythm. "Awn-droh-saw-kay calm-eye-jaws-may."

Holly tried to say it, slowly and awkwardly at first, but with more of a beat the second time. Soon she could roll it off her tongue as well as Michael could. Both of them laughed.

"Now, smell them," Dad said, smiling.

Holly bent down. "They smell good!"

"Yeah, like jasmine, I guess." Michael looked almost comical, with his grin and black eye, bending over to smell the flowers.

The last thing you'd ever get me to do was stick my bum up in the air to smell any flowers. But, curious, I reached down to pick one. The flower stalk didn't break off, though. Instead, the whole thing came up in my hand with a miniature root, a small wreath of spiked leaves and five tiny furry white flowers on a narrow red stem.

"You should never pick wildflowers," said Michael.

The plant hung from my hand. "Don't be crazy, there are hundreds of them."

"There won't be if everybody picks them." Why did

he have to sound so sad? No longer wanting to find out what it smelled like, I flung the little plant away and scowled at Michael.

After lunch we rode for some time without speaking. Suddenly Duke raised his head and pointed his ears forward. Muggs, too, had noticed something. And then we saw it. A huge cow elk, just like in calendar pictures. She stood at the edge of the meadow watching us for what seemed to be minutes but was probably only seconds. I hardly dared breathe. Even the horses stood as though hypnotized.

The elk stared from one of us to the other, back and forth, as though she were trying to read our minds. Then, elegantly, she turned and walked into the forest.

I wanted to follow her. That big animal was the first living thing I'd ever seen that seemed to be independent of human beings, above us, outside our influence. She didn't even seem afraid of us. Sure, if we had yelled or shot at her, she would have disappeared immediately into the forest. But the way she had been standing there, elegant and aloof, it was obvious that we didn't really matter to her. She looked totally different from an elk in a zoo, as though she owned the world.

Even when we rode on, the memory of those free, untameable eyes stayed with me. Maybe that was why people went to the mountains. And maybe that was why some hunters came home happy even if they didn't shoot anything. Maybe they didn't *want* to shoot anything, just needed to see big, free wild creatures . . .

We were riding along the river. Holly broke the silence. "What if Patches isn't in this valley?"

"He has to be," Dad said. "Nobody has seen him

anywhere on the trail that leads to the staging area. And there's no way he'd stay up at the lake all by himself. He's probably hiding somewhere in the trees or little meadows on either side of this valley."

Holly bent her head and looked away.

"Tell you what," Dad said, "let's split up. We can cover more ground that way. Greg and Holly, you keep searching the hills along this side of the river. It's nice easy riding all the way. Some of the trails along the other side are a lot steeper. They're not used as much, so there's lots of deadfall and a few dangerous places where the banks have crumbled away. We two old mountain men better search over there." He grinned.

"What if something happens when we're riding on our own?" Holly asked.

"Just holler," Dad said. "We'll hear you and come racing over here, don't worry. Otherwise we'll meet you back at camp about six."

Nine

Dad and Michael rode across the river and soon disappeared into the trees. Holly and I continued following the trail along "our" side of the river. Duke kept whinnying and looking across the river for his friends, Lightning and Muggs. We could hear their answering whinnies from somewhere in the forest. Finally Duke gave up and strode ahead. Bud pranced to keep pace.

I kept thinking about Dad and Michael. They'd be talking together as they rode. It had been years since Dad and I had done anything together, just the two of us. And we never really talked anymore. Michael could have stayed with Holly. Dad could have taken me over to the other side to ride with him.

Holly was watching me. "I'm sorry you hate this so much."

"I don't see why I have to like it. I'm here. I do the driving because nobody else has a license . . ."

"I have a license," she said.

"So why didn't you drive?" It seemed strange to imagine her handling a big truck pulling a stock trailer full of horses. Holly probably could have done it, though, I realized.

"My dad would never let me drive his precious truck."

"Why not?"

"My parents worry about me all the time," Holly said. "They'd never sleep if I was hauling horses on mountain roads. You wouldn't believe how much convincing your dad had to do before they even let me come along this week. If it were up to my parents I'd never get on a trail ride. 'The mountains are much too dangerous!'"

"If they don't want you to do anything dangerous, how come they let you ride in the truck with *me*?" I said snidely.

She looked embarrassed. "Well, they didn't, actually. They told me I had to ride with your dad."

"Oh?" I tried to suppress a grin. Even this girl, was she after me, too? "So how come you wanted to ride with me?"

Holly turned and looked me straight in the eye. "Maybe I was just curious, wondering what all these other girls see in you. Anyway, my parents worry about me too much. They never want to let me do anything."

"How come?"

She was twisting the reins in her hands. "Oh, they're just really protective." Her voice had become mournful. There was something else, more than what she was saying. But this was getting too heavy for me. Best to keep conversations with girls light and pleasant. You never knew what they might dump on you.

The forest opened into a small meadow full of wild-flowers. Last night Holly had listened to me. Now I could listen to her. The trouble was, she looked sad enough to start crying. I never knew what to do when girls cried. So I pointed to some thick gray clouds building over the mountains. "Bet it's going to rain."

"Probably. But aren't the colors great?" She smiled then. "Those dark purple clouds hanging over the blue-gray mountains, all the different greens of the grasses and trees, the blues and pinks and yellows of those flowers . . . I wish I had my oil paints out here."

"I didn't know you painted."

"I'm not what you'd call an artist." She laughed. "But I have fun smearing bright colors over canvas. You'd hate it, Greg. Oil paints are gooey and messy."

"Yeah, give me math anytime," I said, ducking under a low branch as the trail led back into the forest.

"It's a special subject, I agree," Holly said, still smiling. "When I sweat over a really hard math prob-lem, working it out step by step all by myself, well, I feel so good."

I thought of how Amanda groaned and giggled about her math homework and how she always tried to con me into doing it for her. Even my best friends figured I was completely crazy to be thrilled about solving tough algebra problems.

We were riding into a larger meadow, this one full of furry pink flowers. A strong wind started to blow. Holly gazed into the distance. "I wish we could figure out where Patches is — logically, the way we would solve a math problem, step by step."

As if to dampen her idea, rain began to pour. When Holly tried to put her slicker on, Bud reared and her sleeve caught her glasses, knocking them to the ground. I jumped down to retrieve them.

"Stupid old glasses," she said. "They never did fit me. Too bad my new ones drowned."

I handed the thick heavy glasses to her. "Did you ever think of getting contact lenses?"

She shook her head and grinned. "Naw, I need glasses to hide behind. Besides, it wouldn't be worth all the trouble for me to have contact lenses. I'd still look ugly."

I felt annoyed at her. "How come you always put yourself down about your looks or your weight?"

"I'm just trying to be funny."

"But you really mean it, don't you?"

She frowned. "Isn't it better to joke about something than to complain or cry? How do you think I feel when I look at slim glamorous girls? I joke that I need to lose weight, but I know I could never change my stocky build — some people are just born with chunky bones."

"Girls worry too much about their looks," I said.

"Oh, sure! And guys like you wouldn't be seen dead with a girl unless she's gorgeous!"

I didn't answer.

She shrugged. "Anyway, lots of guys worry about their looks, too. How do you think Michael feels being in the shadow of a brother like you? He's pretty good-looking, but I'll bet he thinks he's ugly when he compares himself to you."

"Not Michael," I said. "He doesn't even think of such things."

"You might be surprised."

"But there are more important things than looks." I could hardly believe what I was saying.

"I know." She laughed. "So that's why I try to make a joke out of it."

I didn't know how to respond, and said nothing. We rode on in silence, but I could tell she wasn't mad at me, and that gave me a peaceful feeling.

It rained most of the afternoon, but there was something cozy about the rain, especially when we were riding through the trees. Most of the time we rode without talking. It felt different to be with someone who wasn't afraid of silence. My friends in Calgary, even the guys, always had to fill every moment with talk or loud music.

We came to an empty camp where a creek tumbled down the rock ledge, making a small waterfall. In the pouring rain we sat on the rocks beside the waterfall, staring at the valley below. I had an orange left in my saddlebag and Holly had a chocolate bar, so we shared them.

Then we wandered along the ledge by a bank of wet sticky clay. Suddenly Holly stopped and crouched low. "Wild strawberries!"

Most of the strawberries lay on the ground, too muddy to eat, but some hung above the leaves. Like babies, we crawled about on our hands and knees, searching for the red rain-washed berries, each one smaller than a baby's fingernail.

In my eagerness I gobbled many a muddy strawberry

and felt the gritty crunch of clay against my teeth. Still, those tiny strawberries tasted sweeter than anything I'd ever known. It was a while before we climbed back on the horses again to continue our search.

The rain had stopped by the time we all met back at camp. It was obvious from their faces that Dad and Michael hadn't found any trace of Patches, either.

We hobbled the horses in the meadow so they could graze while we cooked supper. All except Lightning, of course.

Steak, onions, carrots and fire-baked potatoes — that was the evening's menu, our last night of fresh meat. From now on it would be canned meat. The steak had thawed but it was still cool.

Michael chose the job of peeling and slicing the carrots. He put them on to boil over the smoky fire, then whistled for Lightning. The horse trotted into camp to gobble peelings.

"A horse doesn't belong in camp," I said.

"He's not hurting anybody."

I clenched my teeth, determined not to lose my cool this time. It seemed as though I were two completely different people, one around Michael, and the other away from him. He brought out the worst in me. I detested the chemical reaction that took control of my body whenever I became mad at Michael. And I hated him for having the power to do it to me. Somehow I had to learn not to let him get to me.

Lightning wandered over to the pack boxes and started sniffing them. Michael grinned and said, "'Yond Cassius has a lean and hungry look.'"

And then I did it again. Despite my best intentions,

I blew up. "You and your stupid Shakespeare!" My voice seemed to echo in my ears.

He stared at me, his eyes wide. "I was just trying to be funny."

"Well, you aren't funny. You just make me sick! And get your horse out of the camp." I couldn't seem to stop.

"He's not hurting anything. He's used to roaming around like this."

Why couldn't Dad stick up for me? But no, he just kept on stirring the onions in the frying pan, moving around the fire every time the wind changed, trying to get away from the eye-stinging smoke.

* * *

After supper we saddled the horses to search some more. Again Dad sent me with Holly to the more level side of the valley so the great cowboys could ride the tougher trails together.

For a few minutes Holly and I rode without saying a word. Then she said, "You don't have to always like Michael."

"You're sure right about that."

"No, I mean, you can love somebody without liking him all the time."

"What are you talking about?" I reined Duke in.

"When Michael says or does something that bugs you —" she pushed her glasses up " — you could give yourself permission to not like him those times."

We had entered another small meadow. Holly's voice gathered momentum. "Then maybe he wouldn't get to you . . ."

Before I had a chance to argue or reply, Holly said,

"Ah, this is getting too complicated. And I talk too much. Race you to that big tree." She loosened Bud's reins. He lunged, then galloped full speed across the meadow, but Duke caught up to him just before we reached the huge pine.

"Old Duke is pretty fast," she said, and then we rode on. Neither of us mentioned anything more about what she had said. But I couldn't get it out of my mind.

* * *

Back at camp that night, Michael said some dumb things as usual, but I told myself that I didn't have to like him all the time. And to my amazement, I found I could laugh instead of getting mad.

We all sat talking like normal human beings, sharing funny stories around the crackling fire. Holly made us cocoa, and grinned when she handed me a cup. Everything seemed so relaxed. Dad and Michael were smiling. Maybe this was going to work.

Even when Michael looked up at the moon and started quoting Shakespeare again — "'How sweet the moonlight sleeps upon this bank,'" — even then I didn't get upset. In fact, I was surprised to realize that his voice really was half joking when he said it, as though he were trying to entertain us rather than to show off.

Ten

It was drizzling the next morning, gray and cold. Dad and Michael tied a tarp in the trees above the pack-box cupboards to shelter us from the rain while we were cooking.

In our plastic raincoats, we swished around, shivering, to make breakfast. By the time we were ready to eat, the rain had stopped. I took off my slicker, draped it over a wet stump and sat down carefully, trying not to groan. Oh, the pain. Horseback riding was destroying my body.

When we were almost finished eating, Michael said, "Hey, I just thought of something! What if Patches went the other way? North from Sky Lake, down into the other valley, toward Cutbank Creek staging area."

Holly speared the last piece of bacon. "Patches always wanted to head home even when I was riding him. He wouldn't go on a new trail in a direction opposite to the one he came in on."

"Not all by himself." Michael's voice rose in

excitement. "But what if he was still at Sky Lake when we left and another group came up from the other side? He'd tag along with them when they went back." Michael waved his fork, hardly noticing the piece of pancake he'd dropped on his boot.

Dad stood up and poured hot water into the rinse pan. "Patches has to be in this valley somewhere. We just have to keep looking."

Michael grabbed a dish towel and stood waiting, wrapping it around his hands as he talked. "I'll bet he followed another group north toward Cutbank Creek."

Dad started gathering dishes. "Michael, he'd head the way he came in. I thought you were such a horse expert."

Just then Lightning sauntered into camp. "Go away." I took a deep breath. "We don't need you around here."

"He's not hurting you," Michael said.

I wondered if it would ever be possible to love him when I felt this way about him. "Please, Michael. Horses don't belong in camp."

Dad squirted detergent into the dishpan. Lightning stood nuzzling Michael. Dad began washing the breakfast dishes, tossing them into the rinse pan. Suddenly Lightning bent his head and started drinking from the rinse water. Michael laughed. "He's thirsty this morning."

Green, grassy slobber from Lightning's lips was mixing with the rinse water around the clean dishes. "Get out of there!" I smashed my fist against the horse's nose. He snorted and scrambled out of the way.

Michael wasn't laughing anymore. "Don't you dare hit my horse!"

"Then keep your bloody horse away from here." My voice rang out across the stillness of the meadow. I cringed and tried to take control of myself. "Please get your horse away from here."

"You always want things your way," Michael yelled. "You had no right to hit my horse."

"My way? You're the one who wants everything your way. You want a horse slobbering in the dishpan. So we're all supposed to accept it. Well, sorry, no sane person would want that."

"Are you calling me insane?" Michael asked, his lips trembling.

"The thought did cross my mind."

"Just because I'm not like you. Maybe you're the insane one, Greg. Always yelling and mad at every little thing —"

"Because you make me hate you so much —"

"Shut up!" Dad lifted his soapy hands from the dishpan, spilling water down his jeans. "I am sick and tired of you guys fighting." His voice cracked. "Because of your fighting, a week in these beautiful mountains has turned into a nightmare."

He was looking only at me while he was saying that. My throat burned and my eyes began to sting. I turned to Michael and snarled, "It's all your fault. I wish you were dead!"

Suddenly Holly was in front of me, her face white and contorted. "Don't you ever say that again. Not ever again." She formed each word slowly, deliberately, her eyes huge and round. For another moment she remained there, eyes burning, clenched fists lifted as though she were going to attack me, then she spun away and ran, crashing through the willows. She tripped and fell, pulled herself up and kept running.

I stood fuming, then stomped off in the opposite direction. Too bad for Holly. So what if she thought I was wrong. She didn't understand me, either. None of them did. Just thinking about it made me angrier. All three of them pouncing on me. And all because I didn't want a horse slobbering in the dishwater.

As I walked, I kept seeing the look in Holly's eyes. It wasn't a look of anger or even hatred. No, it had been pain, raw, naked agony. Those eyes kept haunting me until my feet turned me around and steered me in the direction she'd taken. I saw her sitting hunched up by the river.

Me apologize? Never. I kept walking, past her, but my feet turned me again and brought me back to the bank where she sat staring across the valley. Her eyes were red and wet, her face hard.

"Holly, I guess I shouldn't have said that."

She didn't answer, just put her head down against her knees.

"Holly, what you were talking about yesterday — about loving Michael without liking him all the time . . ."

Still she wouldn't look at me.

"It sounds good," I said, sitting down beside her on the cold ground. "Caring about a person without having to like everything he does. Sounds like a great idea." I was getting angry again. "But, Holly, it isn't as easy as it sounds. You'd never understand how awful it can be to have a brother —"

"I had a brother."

My mouth dropped open. "You what?"

"I had a brother." She lifted her head and gazed toward the mountains.

I sat, unable to speak.

She started again, her voice brittle. "Jonathan. Five years ago . . . he died. When he was ten and I was eleven. When we were living in Edmonton."

"How?" I could hardly get my breath.

"Car accident. He was with my aunt. Somebody hit the side of her car."

I cringed. And I had said I wished my brother were dead. "Oh, Holly, I'm sorry . . ."

She leaned her head against my shoulder. Just for a moment she held it there, but when I tried to put my arm around her, she pulled away and stared at the river. My heart was pounding louder than it had ever pounded before. And my throat ached.

Then she started talking again, her voice flat. "That morning — the last morning I ever saw him — we had a big fight because he had used my felt pens. He loved to draw cartoons with felt pens. But he always forgot to put the caps back on, and they'd dry up. Then he'd use mine. He'd forget to put the caps back on them too . . ."

She shivered. "Jonathan lived a few days after the accident, but they wouldn't let me see him. They said it would give me nightmares. I needed to tell him I was sorry. So I put all my felt pens in my pocket and took the bus to the hospital. I was going to sneak in, but a nurse caught me. So I never got to tell him."

I sat dumbstruck. I had wished my brother dead. And sometimes brothers did die. I could still feel the place on my shoulder where Holly's head had rested. Count-less girls had put their heads on my shoulder, but I'd never felt shaky like this before. It had to be from the cold . . .

She clenched her hands. "If he could be alive again, I'd buy millions and millions of felt pens and he could use them all whenever he liked and leave the caps off every one of them."

She leaned her head against her knees again. "Mom and Dad never talk about Jonathan, not even to me. And ever since he died, they've been scared to let me out of their sight.

"Jonathan," she said in a voice so low I could hardly hear it. Then she turned to me. "I loved his name. You know the story of David and Jonathan in the Bible? They weren't even related, but they were like brothers. Like brothers should be."

I winced.

"In the Bible story Jonathan saved David's life many times . . ." She picked a small yellow wildflower from the bank and held it cupped in her hand. "I used to get mad at Jonathan a lot. I can't even remember why now. One day when we were little I yelled at him and chased him away when he tried to follow me. When I came home, Jonathan was sitting on the steps, crying, with a fistful of dandelions he'd picked for me. They were already wilted, but I put them in a jam jar and kept them in my room until the water turned rotten."

I still hadn't found any words to say.

She sat silent for a few more minutes, then sighed. "I guess we'd better get on with our search." She stood up. "You know, sometimes I don't think I'll ever see Patches again, either."

* * *

When we got back to camp we found that Michael and Dad had left with their horses. We saddled our mounts and headed down the valley after them. Soon, we could see them far ahead, riding up and down the hills, in and out of the trees.

I glanced at Holly, riding beside me, quiet and sad. She'd smile when we found her horse. Then I shuddered. *If* we found him. Maybe he had run off with the wild horses. Lost. Like Jonathan — never to be seen again.

We caught up to Michael and Dad. They had stopped where the trail took off for Sky Lake. "Please," Michael was saying, "let's go up and search the north valley. Please."

"It would waste the whole day." My father's voice sounded tired.

"But, Dad," Michael said, "we searched this valley last week and all day yesterday. Besides, if he's around here, why hasn't he wandered into camp to visit our horses? They're his friends. He'd hear them whinny and he'd come for a visit."

I had never heard Michael and Dad argue like that before.

Even when we split up to search the forested hills, Holly and I could hear them arguing across the valley, but neither of us said anything about it.

I was glad just to be away from the two of them. The

silence was so peaceful that I was surprised when Holly spoke. "Both Jonathan and I learned to ride on Patches," she said quietly, almost as though talking to herself. "He was like our baby-sitter. One day we discovered that Patches loved to have his lips scratched. From then on, Patches would lean his head against us and wave his big, flabby old lips, trying to get us to scratch them."

We met Dad and Michael by the river. It wasn't quite noon, but we decided we'd eat our lunch since we were together.

Afterward, as we climbed on our horses, Michael said, "Dad, let's go look in the north valley."

My father shook his head. "There isn't enough time left today. It would take hours just to get there."

"Then let's do it tomorrow."

"And waste another whole day? Can't you see we're running out of time?" Dad looked around. "Tell you what, let's ride directly to the big campsite at the south end of this valley. Somebody's probably camping there, and might have seen him on the way in. Who knows, Patches might even have followed them all the way there."

"It's a three-hour ride to the south end of Forbidden Valley," said Michael. "*That* would waste the rest of the day."

Dad clenched his reins. "Not as much as searching for him way up on the top of a mountain . . ."

Michael said quietly, "I'm heading for Sky Lake. I'm going to ride down that north trail, and I'm going to do it right now. Holly, will you come with me? So you can catch him. Please." I'd never heard Michael sound so determined.

Holly glanced from Dad to Michael, jerking on Bud's reins as he pranced on the spot like some kind of circus horse. "Patches always knew the way home."

"So where is he?" Michael asked.

She pushed up her glasses and looked at Dad.

I shifted my sore butt in the saddle, thinking of the elk we had seen the day before. Why couldn't I be free like that elk? Get away from all this. Holly's brother had died. Dad and Michael arguing, my anger at Michael . . . I needed to get away from everything.

"Michael, we can't waste a day on some wild-goose chase." Dad sounded very tired.

Michael closed his eyes. "Come on, Holly. Come with me." She didn't answer. He turned Lightning and headed up the trail.

"Michael!" Dad yelled. "Michael, get back here!"

But he rode on, straight in the saddle, his shoulders squared.

Eleven

Dad leaned forward, his face flushed, his hands gripping the saddle horn. "Michael," he bellowed. "Michael Kepler, you get back here!" But my brother kept riding.

I had never seen my father so angry. He lifted his fist and smashed it against the saddle. "Michael!" he shouted.

Still Michael kept riding.

Dad's jaw jutted out, his eyes narrowed. "Go with him, Greg. Get him to come back."

"Why me? Why should *I* go after him?"

He gritted his teeth. "He's scared of you."

"Holly could do it."

"No. I need Holly here when I find Patches."

I wanted to ask him what Michael and I would do if *we* found Patches and couldn't catch him, but I didn't dare. All I managed was, "But, Dad, —"

The muscles in his cheeks tightened into knots. "Greg — bring your brother back."

I urged Duke into a gallop and caught up to Michael. "Holly should have come along," he mumbled as I slowed beside him.

"Well, sorry, you've got me." I shook my head. "I'm supposed to make you come back."

Michael didn't answer. Lightning was already prancing, and Michael kicked him into a trot.

"Boy, is Dad ever mad at you!" I said. It was hard not to smile.

He looked up. "Well, you don't have to sound so thrilled."

"Why not? It's a big event! Good enough for newspaper headlines. FATHER MAD AT YOUNGEST SON FIRST TIME EVER." I laughed, expecting him to be annoyed, but he laughed, too.

He slowed Lightning to a walk, then with his reins in one hand, spread out another imaginary newspaper headline and pretended to read it. "FATHER FORGIVES SON WHEN HORSE FOUND."

I chuckled, but Michael wasn't smiling anymore. "Trouble is," he said, "we won't be able to catch Patches when we do find him."

We splashed through the river and up the trail toward Sky Lake. "What makes you so bloody sure he's down in the other valley?" I asked.

"I just know. I might not know about anything else, but I know about horses." We headed into thick spruce forest, hooves thudding on the needle-covered path. A squirrel zipped along a branch, then stopped suddenly and sat scolding us.

The trail became really steep. Digging their hooves in, heads low, the horses gasped for breath, sweat darkening their necks and shoulders. Lightning certainly wasn't prancing anymore.

A fog moved in, enveloping us. The higher we climbed, the thicker the fog became. Michael frowned. "We won't be able to see the view from up there."

"What a tragedy," I said, grinning. "I don't know if I can survive without seeing the view. Anyway, I'm supposed to be bringing you back. How can I talk you into turning around?"

He didn't smile. The trail leveled out a bit and he turned to me, although his eyes wouldn't meet mine. "Greg . . ." His voice was low. "Greg, I have to tell you something."

"What?"

"Patches escaped because . . . because I lied to Dad. Dad's covering for me and I hate it." He gulped and spoke faster. "So that's why I *have* to find him."

"What are you talking about?" We were riding on the open grassy edge of a hill now. Duke tried to take the lead, but I pulled him in so the horses were walking abreast. "What are you talking about?" I asked again.

Michael stared at the ground. "When Dad left me to finish bringing the horses in that night, I forgot to hobble Patches, and then we got talking for a while around the camp fire . . ."

"We all know that. So, what do you mean about lying?"

"When we were in our sleeping bags, almost asleep, Dad asked me if I'd remembered to hobble Patches and I . . . I lied. I said I had hobbled him when I really hadn't. I lied because I was tired and didn't feel like getting up again."

I exploded. "We're out here riding all over the Rocky Mountains for a whole week because you didn't feel like getting up?"

Head and shoulders bent, Michael trotted Lightning ahead into the fog. Dad had kept the real story from us. The more I thought about it, the angrier I got. I caught up to Michael. "Dad sure wouldn't cover for me if I lied to him. He never cares about me at all."

"Hah," Michael sputtered. "Dad always plays up to you. When he says anything to anybody, he always watches for your reaction."

"Don't be stupid. You've always been his pet and you know it."

"Well, he sure wasn't happy with me when he found Patches' hobbles hanging from the tree the next morning." Michael bit his lip and urged Lightning to trot into the lead again.

Back in the forest, the trail grew even steeper than before. Within minutes we had to stop the horses so they could catch their breath. Duke's sides heaved, moving my knees in and out, in and out. I rolled my eyes as Michael took oats from his pocket and bending low in his saddle, offered the grain to Lightning.

Michael glanced up at me. "If only I dared tell Holly how Patches really escaped . . ." His voice sounded thin and shaky. "Anyway, now you know why I absolutely have to find her horse."

I didn't answer. We reached a fork in the trail. Michael pointed. "That way leads straight up to the top of the ridge. But there's no use riding along there today because we won't be able to see anything. We might as well stay here on the lower trail."

"Thank God for small mercies," I said. The air had become colder and much damper. I put on my jacket and then my raincoat. It was starting to drizzle, but Michael made no effort to put his raincoat on.

The trail continued to climb. We had to stop again to let the horses catch their breath. Soon we entered another clearing. Michael pulled Lightning to a walk beside Duke, then spoke in a strange low voice. "What do you think she thinks of me?"

I glanced at him. "Who?"

"Holly, of course."

I noticed with a shock that his knuckles were white around his reins. And all of a sudden it hit me like a sledgehammer. "Holly? Michael, are you interested in Holly?"

His face flushed and he looked away. Suddenly I remembered one evening when I was a little kid and my pet turtle had fallen off the table and landed on his back with his soft side up and his legs flailing. Michael looked like that now, vulnerable.

"Michael . . ." I was scared by how squeaky my voice came out. "Why Holly? If you want a girlfriend, why not look for one who's cute and has a good figure —" I stopped myself, thinking of how it would hurt Holly to hear me say that.

"There's something special about Holly," Michael said. Then he spoke quickly, almost harshly. "How do you think she feels about me?"

"I'm sure she thinks you're great. She hates it when we fight. So she must think you're worth getting along with."

We were staring at each other like never before, open

and level. Michael looked away first. He muttered, "Don't ever tell her I asked." He sounded so fragile.

"Don't worry." I hesitated. "Uh, how long have you felt this way about her?"

Michael fidgeted with his reins. "Quite a while. Maybe a few months."

I shook my head.

He spoke more softly. "I need to know how she really feels about me. For the past few months, instead of getting closer, it seems as though we can't talk the way we used to when we first started riding together at her place." He frowned. "It seems lately as though we just talk about stupid things — about nothing. Like she feels awkward around me."

"Maybe it's because you're feeling nervous around her."

He nodded. "Yeah."

I straightened my shoulders and took a deep breath. It felt good to talk with my brother like this.

We were riding on a rocky trail now, past smaller, scruffier trees. A few minutes later there were no trees at all. Just the heavy gray fog and a solid brown mountain wall all the way along one side of the trail. Not even one tiny tree.

"Timberline," said Michael. "If it were a clear day you'd be able to see right down to our camp from here."

I'd learned about the timberline in school, about how trees couldn't grow above a certain altitude, but I hadn't expected it to be so dramatic. Trees, and then suddenly no trees at all.

My thoughts were racing. Michael and Holly? The truth was that she never seemed the least bit interested in him. But then, I hadn't been watching, had I? Or was it that I was hoping she might be interested in me? I pushed that thought out of my head, annoyed to even consider it.

Poor Michael. What if Holly didn't want him? It would destroy my brother.

When I was in grade one and madly in love with the girl who sat in front of me, I tried to kiss her at recess one day. She pulled away, glaring, which hurt worse than if she'd hit me. But the next afternoon another pretty girl smacked me on the arm with a rolled-up piece of paper, then ran giggling and blushing into the girls' washroom. My ego had mended quickly.

Poor Michael just didn't have it with girls. They never phoned him, never paid attention to him. But he hadn't ever seemed interested in them, either.

Shocked, I realized that I was actually worrying about my brother for the first time since I could remember. Maybe I was going crazy from this trip. But he looked so pathetic with the colorful bruises around those sad serious eyes.

We rode without talking. My whole body hurt, and my head was churning. Michael liked Holly. And Michael had lied. Did Holly like Michael? Dad had covered for Michael. Holly's brother had died. And my heart had pounded when Holly put her head against my shoulder. This week was turning out to be much too complicated.

The horses' shoes rattled through loose gray rocks as the trail narrowed. Short scruffy grass and a few wildflowers stuck up here and there along the edge. The fog enclosed us like a wall. I was almost curious about the view, but no way would I admit that to Michael.

To my surprise the trail turned down again. Duke skidded on the steep path, stumbling on the loose rocks. "Lean back in your saddle," Michael said. "It's easier for your horse."

Soon we were into trees again, but still moving downward. At a second fork, Michael said, "If we'd ridden up along the ridge, here's where we'd have come out again."

The forest became thicker and the trail gradually leveled out as we passed through a couple of small grassy meadows.

When we headed out of the forest and up a sharp slope, I hunched over against the wind, wishing for my heavy jacket. The horses fought the hill, then finally we were at the top. Michael pointed to a ghostly outline towering far above us. "Barricade Mountain," he said. He lowered his hand. "Sky Lake is down there. But we can't see anything in this stupid fog, so we might as well keep going."

On the other side of the hill we rode almost immediately back into forest. I took a deep breath, glad to be sheltered from the wind.

Without warning Michael stopped Lightning. All around us trees stood like ghosts. Suddenly I realized we were in a campsite. "Is this where Patches got away?" I asked.

"Yeah." Head bent, Michael pointed to a big spruce. "That's the tree I tied him to."

"Shouldn't we look around here a bit?" I asked.

"Naw, Dad's right about that. A horse would never stay up here by himself so many days. We might as well head for the north valley right away."

It was nearly three o'clock. I thought about asking if we could get off to stretch our legs, but seeing Michael's set jaw, I knew he wouldn't be in any mood to stop. We rode back out of the forest and headed almost straight up, north along a narrow rocky track.

When the trail leveled out, we rounded a corner, hugging the mountainside, then came to a tiny meadow with a bubbling spring and lush green grass.

We did stop then, to have a drink of water, the most delicious water I'd ever tasted. I bent over, leaning on soft moss, taking great gulps. Our horses, too, slurped from the spring, not at all eager to leave. Michael gave Lightning another handful of oats, climbed on and sat waiting for me.

Down we rode, down, down, the horses' hooves skidding on the loose rocks, and then the forest closed in again.

My body could hardly remember how it felt not to be in pain. This was Tuesday. My third day of riding out here. You'd think I'd be getting used to it by now. But we'd been spending more and more hours in the saddle each day.

Finally the trail became level, gradually at first, downward still, but not nearly so frightening. The fog thinned and the air felt warmer. I took off my raincoat.

The trail was soft dirt again. On we rode, through a few more small grassy clearings. The sky was still cloudy, but we could see far below us into a long green valley. Our eyes scanned the edges of the forest. No sign of a horse. Neither of us had spoken for some time, but that old familiar chemical reaction was starting to brew inside my guts.

"Michael," I finally called, "this is absolutely ridiculous. Obviously the horse isn't here. Dad was right."

"We didn't see him in Forbidden Valley, either, did we?" asked Michael quietly.

"It's almost five. We have to head back."

"We should be close to a camp," said Michael.

"What makes you think that? I thought you'd never been down in this valley before."

"I haven't. But there's usually a camp every couple of hours of riding. We can still make it back before dark."

"We'll be a bit hungry by then."

"We can stop for a break," he said. "I have two oranges and some chocolate bars in my saddlebag."

"Always prepared."

He didn't answer.

Just when I was getting ready to strangle him, Michael stopped Lightning by a creek, dug around in his saddlebag and threw me an orange. We sat on the rocks peeling our oranges. "Michael," I said, "it's almost six o'clock. Nearly five hours back now."

"The horses will move faster headed toward home. We can't come all this way and not find him. We could be so close. Just another few minutes. Please."

"I think you need a brain transplant!"

Instead of frowning or turning away, he laughed.

In the ice-cold creek water I rinsed sticky orange juice off my hands, but had totally given up on the idea of actually getting clean. My head was all sweaty from the thick cowboy hat, and my hair felt as if someone had combed cooking oil into it. Moving my arms, I smelled sour perspiration. If my friends were here to see and smell me now, I'd die.

Then I smiled to myself. If my friends were here, they'd look and smell just as bad! Imagining Amanda or Ken in this condition was enough to make me laugh.

Struggling back onto Duke, I wondered how I'd manage to ride all the way back to camp that night without collapsing.

"Michael, how come you never get saddle sore?" I asked when we were down in the valley.

"I guess I'm just used to riding. And they say the more relaxed you are, the less sore or stiff you get."

"So if I took a tranquillizer, I'd be more relaxed and less sore." We both laughed. "Remind me to get a prescription next time."

The trail led us through a couple of small meadows, across a river, then a little while later, into a huge meadow. And there, across the clearing, stood three big stained-canvas tents. A few hobbled horses lifted their heads and whinnied to us.

"So there was a camp," I said. "How does it feel to always be right?"

"I thought I was always wrong," Michael said. "At least that's how you make me feel." Our eyes locked for a moment. I looked away.

Smoke curled from the chimney of the biggest tent. "Anybody there?" Michael called. A woman emerged, smiling, wooden spoon in hand.

"Don't suppose you've seen a stray pinto gelding around?" Michael asked.

"Matter of fact, we have."

Twelve

"Where?" Michael asked without even glancing back to say that he'd told me so. "Where did you see this horse?"

"Oh, he's around here somewhere." The woman gestured with her wooden spoon. "Or maybe he followed my husband and the dudes to Spruce Falls this morning. Last Friday when we were at Sky Lake, he followed us back here. That was just before the blizzard. He's been hanging around ever since. Is he yours?"

"He belongs to this girl we know," Michael answered, "but it's my fault he got loose."

"Well," she said, "we've tried everything we could think of to catch him. And he's getting sneakier and sneakier."

"Only Holly can catch him," said Michael. "She's the girl who owns him. She can always catch him."

"Yeah," I added, "and she's with our dad at the far end of Forbidden Valley looking for him. We'll have to ride all the way back here with her tomorrow."

The woman crossed her arms. "I don't know. About seven tomorrow morning we're riding out to Cutbank Creek, and we won't be back until Friday. That old pinto might follow us out or find some other horses to latch on to."

That made me sit up. "You mean we have to catch him tonight?"

The woman thought for a moment. "Maybe you could take the chance that he does follow us out. You could all drive to Cutbank Creek to meet us so the girl could catch him there."

"That's a great idea," I said before Michael had a chance to open his mouth. Then we could head straight back to Calgary! I couldn't believe my luck.

The woman interrupted my thoughts, her voice slow. "Only one problem. We can't wait long — our dudes have to catch a plane in Calgary. So you'll have to be at the staging area by noon for sure."

"I don't know," said Michael. "If the least thing goes wrong, we won't be at Cutbank Creek in time. Then Patches would be left wandering. Not a good idea . . ."

"Nothing would happen," I said. "He'll hang around and we'll find him there."

Michael put on his stubborn voice. "He might follow another group back in. Or he might not follow you all the way out." He looked around. "No, we'll have to get him tonight."

"Michael, you've flipped your lid. We can't catch Patches without Holly, and we don't even know whether he went with the others up the trail or if he's hanging around down here somewhere."

Michael turned to the lady. "Which way is Spruce Falls?"

She pointed south toward a treed hill at the foot of a mountain. "Go back to the last meadow, and you'll find a trail leading off to the right up into the trees."

Michael nodded. "Patches would follow your husband's horses up the hill. But where the trail becomes really steep, he'd give up and head back."

She grinned. "You know horses, eh? By the way, Madge Galleger's my name. Mac — that's my husband — and I run this here camp."

Michael gestured at me. "My brother, Greg. I'm Michael. Michael Kepler. So, Patches is probably somewhere on the falls trail." His eyes were shining. "When do you expect your group back? Maybe there'd be enough people to surround him."

"Problem is, they won't be in any hurry," Madge said. "This is their last night here, so they'll want to stay out as long as possible. And I sent lots of food along, so they probably won't be home until dark. By then you won't even be able to see your pinto, let alone catch him."

"So we'll have to look for him now," Michael said.

My temper flared. "There's no use looking for a horse we can't catch. It's almost six-thirty. It's going to take us until midnight as it is to get back to camp. And I don't like the idea of riding those steep trails in the dark."

He was staring at me, so I continued. "What if we get up real early tomorrow morning and ride in here with Holly? If we don't see Patches around here, we can ride on to Cutbank Creek."

Michael shook his head, turned Lightning and headed up the hill away from us.

"Michael!"

He stopped for a moment and turned in the saddle. "You go back if you want. How do you think Holly would feel if we were this close and didn't even try to get him?

"How do you think you'll catch him, you idiot?"

"I will — somehow. Don't you worry."

He touched his heels to Lightning and trotted off.

I looked at Madge. She shrugged. I could ride back alone. But there were rivers to cross. There might be bears. Anything could happen and there'd be no one to go for help.

But Michael didn't mind the idea of riding on his own. So why should I?

"I guess I'll head back," I muttered.

Madge frowned. "It's none of my business, but if I was you, I'd go with him. He'll need all the help he can get. I'd come and help, too, except I've got bread baking in my old stove."

Fuming, I looked at my brother's straight stubborn back and turned Duke to follow him. Michael, I hate you, I thought, and would have shouted it right out loud if that woman hadn't been standing there.

I lagged behind to avoid talking to Michael as we rode back to the meadow and followed a steep narrow trail into the forest.

Suddenly Michael stopped and swiveled in his saddle to look at me. "It's Patches," he whispered, grinning like a madman.

I couldn't see anything at all, but my heart started pounding.

Then I heard a branch swish and sure enough there was a fat swaybacked pinto peering at us through the trees. And yes, there was a marking on his head, a white marking that resembled a crooked number seven.

"Now what?" I whispered.

Michael lowered himself to the ground, handed me Lightning's reins and crept toward Patches. "Good boy. Just stay there, Patches. Everything's okay."

I could hardly breathe. It looked as though Michael was going to pull this off after all. We'd take Patches back with us tonight. This was unbelievable.

"It's okay, Patches," he crooned. "Don't worry." The horse stood as though hypnotized. Michael was only an arm's length away. Then, slowly and deliberately as a cat, he raised his arm toward Patches' halter ring.

That was all it took. The horse swung away, crashing through the trees, then stopped far from us. His brown-and-white markings were an effective camouflage in the sun-dappled shade of the spruce forest.

Michael approached Patches again, even more slowly this time, murmuring gently. But when he came close, Patches spun away.

One more time he tried, but he'd moved only a few footsteps before Patches bolted. Michael's face twisted as though in pain. "Holly, why didn't you believe me?" he whispered.

"Don't you have oats in your pocket?" I asked.

"No. There's none left. Besides, it wouldn't help." Michael sighed. "Last week we tried for almost an hour to catch him with oats. He'd just snatch a mouthful and lunge away every time we tried to grab his halter."

My brother took his lariat off the saddle and started walking toward Patches again. Michael was pretty good at roping fence posts. But as soon as the lariat came at him, Patches snorted and lurched off into the trees.

Michael coiled his lariat, crept near the horse and threw it once more. But, as before, Patches jumped away the moment the rope left Michael's hand.

Again he gathered his rope and headed for the pinto. I stood with my hands on my hips. "Michael, you're so dumb! Can't you see when something isn't working?"

He spun around, waving his fist at me. "Quit putting me down!" Startled, Patches bolted off into the trees.

For sure Patches would escape if we kept this up. "Michael . . ."

"What?" He glared at me.

"You . . . We . . . we're doing this all wrong," I said softly.

His face relaxed. "What do you suggest?"

"I don't know."

"If only we had a bunch of people," my brother said in a flat voice. "We could surround him."

The idea hit me then. "Hey, what if we surround him with your lariat? We could go back down the trail and thread your rope between the trees where they're really thick, to make a little open-ended corral across the path. Then if we could get him to follow the trail down the hill, we could trap him in it."

I was getting excited. "We could tie our horses on

the other side of the trap. Patches might be so interested in them he wouldn't notice the rope."

Michael's eyes widened and then he grinned. "You know, Greg, you're not as dumb as you look."

Thirteen

We led our horses down the hill until we were out of Patches' sight, then started threading Michael's lariat around the trees and across the trail. But the rope wasn't long enough to make even three-quarters of the circle we needed.

"Now what?" Michael asked.

"Our reins. They'll do." We unclipped the reins from our bridles and tied our animals with their halter ropes. Joining four leather reins to the lariat gave enough length to complete our tiny corral.

"One of us will have to hide right here," I said, "to close the trap across the trail the minute he steps in. And to grab his halter right away before he gets any idea of charging out. We probably have just one chance to try this trick."

Michael beamed. "You're starting to think like a horse."

"Oh, no!" I wrinkled my face. "Hey, Michael, remember the time you tied Duke with his bridle and reins instead of his halter rope?"

"Sure do. When I was about five. Duke pulled back and broke the beautiful leather reins Mom had just bought Dad for his birthday. I'll never forget how mad Dad was!" He grinned. "See, Dad does get mad at me. Today wasn't the only time."

"So it's twice. Poor little Michael." But we were chuckling and our banter felt good.

"Which one of us stays here?" Michael asked.

"You'd better. He knows you, so he won't panic after you've grabbed him."

"He won't panic after anybody grabs him," Michael said. "He's really a friendly tame horse. It's just that he doesn't want to be caught. Once we get hold of his halter, he'll behave perfectly. But I'll stay here if you want."

Leaving Michael with the horses, I crept through the trees to move up and around Patches.

When I was well above the pinto on the side away from the trail, I started strolling toward him, talking gently, my hands out as though I were trying to catch him. Sure enough he turned from me, onto the trail and down the hill toward our trap.

I had to take it easy or he'd start running. I stopped to let him nibble a few blades of grass, then slowly headed for him again. He walked away from me, another few steps down the trail.

Again I stopped. He stared at me suspiciously. I looked away, let him relax, then started toward him, but in my excitement I walked too fast. Off the trail he trotted, into the trees.

I took a deep breath. I'd have to sneak up the side of the hill and then around to head him back in the direction of the trail. Even I knew that horses always preferred to walk on a trail.

Twigs snapped beneath my feet no matter how quietly I tried to move. At every snap, Patches moved farther away from me, away from the trail.

I climbed until I couldn't see the horse any longer, then once more sneaked across the hill. Now I'd have to be careful not to spook him by popping back into sight.

Through the underbrush I crept, watching for Patches, not noticing the branch sticking out waiting to trip me. I fell hard, sliding down the mossy hill.

I lay sprawled on the ground, letting the pain subside, and became aware of the heavy sweet smell of spruce. My left arm and wrist hurt the most. But I could flex them in all the right places, so I hadn't broken any bones.

A bird called high above my head. A squirrel chattered loudly, darting back and forth on a branch like a movie in fast forward. I looked up and saw clouds moving past, exposing a patch of blue sky, circled by a frame of pointed spruce trees.

Around me was moss, green and spongy. I put my face into its softness, smelling the pleasant mustiness. Despite the chatter of the squirrel, an unbelievable quiet filled the forest. I thought of Calgary, the noisy traffic, the heavy smell of exhaust, even the din of a party. Maybe it wasn't so bad out here.

Michael would be wondering what had happened to me. Reluctantly I forced my exhausted aching body to stand up and move on.

My wrist throbbed. I watched the ground more carefully, sneaking along to the other side of Patches, then down the hill.

By the time I saw the crafty old horse he had already noticed me. Head up, ears forward, he stared. I had come out at just the right place, above and far enough to the side so he'd have to move toward the trail.

Then he snorted and looked beyond me into the trees. What if he dashed right past me in the opposite direction? "Please, Patches, please, just be a nice horse and go down the trail." I shook my head. What would my friends think of their pal Greg out here sniffing moss and talking to a horse?

Holding my breath, I sauntered toward Patches. To my relief he turned in the direction of the trail. I felt like laughing and crying as he reached the path and headed toward our trap.

At the crest of the hill, he stopped, turned and looked at me as though he suspected something. I stood as nonchalantly as possible, not even daring to meet his eyes. He took a couple of steps off the trail and stopped, ready to bolt into the trees again. This wasn't going to work. My stomach knotted.

Then one of our horses whinnied. Patches swung around, back on the trail and trotted over the hill. I walked behind him as fast as I dared. When he came in sight of our horses, he stopped and whinnied to them. I could hardly breathe. Our horses nickered again, calling him, and Patches continued down the trail toward them.

Now where was Michael? I couldn't see him

anywhere. What if he messed all this up by not being in the right place?

But the moment Patches walked into our trap, Michael sprung out from behind a big spruce, grabbed the loose end of one rein and flung it around a tree to complete the circle.

Patches pivoted but Michael grabbed his halter. "Gotcha."

I grabbed a rein to put in Patches' halter ring so we could hold him until we sorted everything out. Michael ducked under the rope and clasped his arms around me. Then we stood pounding each other on the back. "We did it, we did it." Michael was almost crying.

Never before had Michael and I hugged each other. Never. It was me who broke away first. We stood as though frozen, saying nothing for a few seconds.

My eyes wouldn't lift to meet Michael's even though I could feel his gaze gentle on me. I reached out to scratch Patches' nose. The old horse bent his head, pushing against my hand.

Then he sighed. Yes, that animal sighed, just like a person enjoying a back rub. And sure enough, when I stopped scratching his nose, Patches stuck out his floppy pink lips and wiggled them, pressing harder against my hand to get me to scratch him again.

Michael and I both laughed. "Hey, how did you know about scratching his lips?" my brother asked. "Holly always does that to him."

I didn't answer, just changed the subject. "How can such a friendly horse be so hard to catch?" I asked.

"Crazy, isn't it?" Michael was grinning from one ear to the other.

I wondered if Holly would be hard to catch too. My heart pounded just thinking of how happy she would be when we rode in with her horse. But I'd never fall for a girl like Holly. She wasn't my type. Besides, Michael was the one who liked her.

I stroked Patches' fat neck. "Well, old fellow," I said, "I guess we'd better get you back to your owner." Then I turned to my brother. "Michael, we did it. We really did it!"

Grinning broadly, Michael nodded. Then he snapped Lightning's halter rope onto Patches and handed it to me. "Here, Greg, you hold him while I take our corral apart. Whatever you do, don't let go of that rope, because for sure we'll never catch him again."

Soon we were riding out, Patches in tow. Every part of my body hurt, I felt dizzy with hunger, but somehow it didn't seem to matter much anymore. We had our horse.

Together we rode, so tired we didn't even talk about our triumph. Over and over I kept thinking about how Holly would smile when she saw Patches. She had a way of smiling with her whole face, eyes sparkling, scrunched almost half shut, the laugh lines going right to her hairline. When Amanda smiled, she never let her whole face scrunch up. Sometimes her smiles looked as cold as ice.

Tomorrow night I'd be at Amanda's place with my friends, helping to decorate. They'd get me to run the streamers from the vaulted cedar ceiling, because I wasn't scared of heights. I'd balance on the tallest step ladder, creating fancy twists and swirls with crepe paper, and the girls would watch in admiration. Getting ready for the party might be even more fun than the party itself. I needed to be sharing in the excitement, back where I really fit, back to where things weren't so mixed-up.

Michael and I stopped for a drink at the creek and watched as the sun slid downward, between the low clouds and the mountaintops, coating everything with a golden light.

We sat sharing Michael's last chocolate bar. It had obviously been in his saddlebag for some time. The chocolate had melted from the heat of the sun, then solidified in the cold air. It looked awful, but I didn't mind. "Great supper," I said, laughing.

"Yeah." Michael handed the wrapper to me. "Here, you can lick the paper." And I did.

We had tied our horses to the trees, but Michael kept Patches with him, holding tightly to his halter rope as the old pinto chewed thick grass around the creek.

"Hey, elephant heads!" Michael shouted. Dragging Patches behind him, my brother scrambled along the muddy bank and knelt in front of some plants. From where I was sitting I could just see tiny pink flowers all along the sides of narrow stalks.

"Look, Greg, perfect elephant heads! See, each one has a little trunk . . ."

I moved closer. "Hey, it's true! An elephant's face. And two floppy ears. Even lips." A dozen or more perfectly formed tiny pink elephants seemed to have raised their trunks, trumpeting along each stalk.

"I won't bother you with their Latin name," said Michael, and we both laughed. "Greg . . ."

"What?"

"I . . . uh . . . it was good you came with me today, you know."

Funny what that did to my insides. "Yeah, we did all right together."

Michael touched his finger to a tiny elephant. "I sure wish Holly could see these. She'd love them."

Then we were on our way again, stopping a few times to let the horses catch their breath. Patches puffed and panted harder than the other two, and it took longer for his breathing to return to normal. "Poor guy," Michael said. "He's sure getting old."

The sun disappeared behind the mountains, turning the clouds to purple, and peaceful darkness took over. A half moon shone faintly through the clouds. The only noise was the thud of hooves as we climbed along the soft dirt trail, and once in a while the hoot of an owl from the trees overhead or the sound of unseen little forest animals scurrying through the underbrush.

When we reached Sky Lake we stopped to give the horses a rest. Their breathing seemed so loud in the darkness. I swung off Duke, my bones crying for relief from pain. Michael stood holding the two horses, reaching under Lightning's neck to scratch Patches on the nose.

"Greg," he said quietly, "I've been thinking. I have to tell Holly the truth. About how Patches really got away. That I was feeling lazy and lied to Dad. I have to tell her."

"Why now?" My chest tightened, thinking about Dad's covering for Michael's lie. Always, no matter what wrong Michael had done, he'd worm his way immediately back into Dad's heart.

"I have to tell her the truth, so I can feel good about myself."

He would worm his way into Holly's heart, too. If he admitted to lying, she'd look at him with wide eyes, admiring him for being so wonderfully honest.

"I can't stand having a lie between us," he added. "Holly is the kind of person who deserves the truth about everything."

That was little Michael, playing up to everybody, trying to get them to think he was so marvelous. He'd end up being the big hero. Michael always wound up smelling like a rose. Me, I was the one who got in trouble even when Michael started it.

"You're sure hung up on Holly," I said, laughing sarcastically. "Quite the little lover boy, aren't you!" I hadn't really meant to say that — it just boiled out.

Michael gulped. "I'm sorry I ever told you," he said, his voice suddenly sharp as a knife. "Nobody should trust you with anything. You're no good, and that's all there is to it."

That really cut deep. I thought of Holly's eyes on me, horrified, when I'd hit Michael by the river. I thought of her eyes when I'd told him I wished he were dead. Michael always provoked me and I ended up looking terrible. Pain and fury mounting, I blurted out the thing I knew would hurt my brother the most. "Yeah, well, Holly probably laughs at you behind your back."

Michael answered, his voice low and deadly, "I'm sure all your so-called friends do too. Nobody could ever really like you. Not even those stupid girls you think adore you so much. Because you aren't anything to like."

Something snapped. "Shut up!" I yelled, lifting my fists and hurling myself at my brother. Lightning jumped back, and Patches spun out of his way, yanking the halter rope from Michael's hand.

Like statues we stood listening to Patches' hooves clatter away into the darkness.

Fourteen

I could hear Michael's gasp and the rattle of Patches' shoes over the rocks, then only silence.

"Head him off!" I cried.

"It's no use." My brother's voice sounded flat and dull, totally lifeless. He slowly climbed on Lightning.

"Michael, where are you going?"

"Back to camp."

"But we have to try . . ."

Again that flat dead voice. "There's no use."

He turned his horse and headed down the trail.

I squinted into the darkness and thought I saw the shape of a horse against some trees. "Michael, he's right here. Please come back. We can figure out something . . ."

No answer. Just the sound of Lightning's hooves moving farther and farther down the trail.

I crept toward the shadow. "Patches, it's okay, Patches." His hooves clattered, running away. Away from Holly.

Defeated, I climbed onto Duke and turned to follow Michael back to camp. Not a single word did we speak the whole way down. The night air had turned desperately cold. Over and over I heard the echo of my loud "Shut up!" and the clatter of Patches' hooves running away.

Just before we reached camp I managed to push some sound past my burning throat. "Michael?"

He looked back at me but said nothing.

"Michael, we wouldn't have to tell them . . ."

He turned his head away.

"Michael, please listen. We could just say we saw him. That's not a lie. We wouldn't have to tell them we had caught him or anything."

Finally my brother spoke, his voice raw with pain. "No. We wouldn't have to."

Dad and Holly came running as they heard us crossing the river. "Michael? Greg?" Dad called, his voice hopeful.

"Yeah, it's us," I answered.

"Thank God," he said.

We climbed the riverbank. "Patches is up by Sky Lake," Michael said slowly.

"You saw him?" Holly cried. "Oh, why didn't I go along? But at least now we know where he is! Thank you. Thank you."

I eased my body off Duke. My knees buckled with pain. Staggering, I led Duke toward the camp fire and held my frozen hands as close as I dared to the flames.

Holly was trembling with excitement, her eyes reflecting the flickering flames. "How did you find him? Talk to me. You guys are wonderful!"

My brother answered, his voice still flat and dead. "He was in the north valley. We . . . thought we had him . . . but he got away. He was behind us as far as the lake." Michael glanced at me, then stared back to the ground. "But he didn't follow us any farther."

"It doesn't matter," she said. "Don't sound so sad. We'll just ride up there tomorrow and I can catch him. At least now we know where he is. I'm so glad you went there!" She really did have beautiful eyes, dark brown and alive behind those thick glasses.

Yellow highlights from the fire played on Michael's thin cheeks, outlining his lips and eyes with deep shadows. He looked as tired as I felt.

Dad turned to Michael. "You were lucky it worked out all right. But don't ever try anything like that again! It's way after midnight. Do you know how dangerous it is to go off alone in the mountains with no food, no gun, no shelter, no extra clothes . . ." He took a deep breath. "We've been worried sick."

My brother, standing beside his horse, winced as though he'd been hit.

Dad looked at Michael, let out his breath, then moved to the fire where he started taking the lids off the pots sitting by the edge of the flames. "You must be starved," he said. The harshness had left his voice. He dished food onto two plates, scraping the bottom of each pot. I took the plates from Dad and handed the fullest one to my brother.

Holly took our horses' reins and stood beside us, watching, waiting as I began shoveling food to my starving stomach. Michael balanced his heaping plate on one hand and poked at a piece of potato with his fork. By the time my plate was empty, Michael had managed to eat only a few bites.

"Hey, Michael," Dad said, "don't worry. You did okay. It's good you went up there. Real good."

Michael took another forkful of food and stood chewing slowly, eyes downcast.

Dad's gaze fixed on him, worried. "Michael, something's really wrong, isn't it?"

Michael chewed more slowly.

Dad took the horses from Holly and led them to the trees to tie them. "Hey," he said, scratching his head, "where's Lightning's halter rope?"

My heart thumped. Michael was staring at his plate. The crackling of the fire seemed so loud it hurt my ears.

"Michael." Dad's voice sharpened. "What happened to Lightning's halter rope?"

"I lost it."

"How?"

Michael looked to me, his eyes wide and desperate. "I can't help it," he said. "It's no use . . ."

"What are you talking about?" Dad asked. "Where is your halter rope?"

"On Patches," Michael said.

I glared at him. "You promised."

"What's going on?" Dad strode toward us.

Michael looked back to me, his lip quivering. "I never promised . . ."

I shook my head. "We didn't have to . . ."

"Maybe you didn't. But I have to . . ."

Both Holly and Dad were standing in front of us, hands on their hips. "You actually caught Patches?" Holly cried.

Michael was glaring at me. "If you didn't always make fun of me . . ."

I stamped my foot. "This time it was *you* putting *me* down —"

"Stop it!" Dad lifted his hands. "You mean, you guys started arguing and lost him? You caught Patches and he got away because you were arguing?"

"He came at me —" Michael said.

The blood pounded in my head. I shouted, "You were deliberately trying to get me upset!"

Dad groaned, clasping his head with both hands.

Then they dragged the story from us, about Madge Galleger, about how we had caught Patches and, of course, the fact that I had lunged at Michael, scaring the horses.

"Boy," said Holly, "you guys really went to a lot of trouble to get me up to Sky Lake."

Suddenly we were laughing, standing there after midnight, laughing like little kids. It helped ease the knot in my stomach, which tightened every time I thought about my friends figuring out who could tape up the streamers tomorrow night and joking about me still being out in the mountains.

But when Dad was putting the saddles away, he mumbled, "I just can't believe it. You guys had to argue . . ." Then we started in all over again, rehashing the whole thing.

"What really worries me," Holly said, "is that Greg heard Patches run down the other side of the hill. What if he went all the way back down into the north valley again? He might follow those people out tomorrow morning . . ."

"It's a long way back to their camp from Sky Lake," Dad said. "And he wouldn't have any horses to follow. No, at least you didn't chase him. So he's probably still hanging around near the lake. Or maybe he followed you guys partway down tonight. Who knows, we might wake up tomorrow morning to find Patches in camp!"

That possibility had never occurred to me. Things were looking up.

"Patches *is* dragging the halter rope," said Michael, sounding more hopeful, too. "He'll keep tripping on it, especially down steep places. That will slow him a lot. He might spend hours just grazing as he wanders down."

"Yeah, it might be a while before he drifts this far," Dad said. "We'll take our time packing in the morning —"

"Packing?" I asked, "couldn't we just ride up for the day?"

"No," said my father. "We might have to stay overnight if we don't find him."

"I'm sure we'll find him. Dad, it'll waste a lot of time packing everything up and making camp again at the lake. If we just ride there early in the morning, we can catch Patches and still have lots of time at Sky Lake. We can stay until late tomorrow night, then head for Calgary Thursday morning. I'd still be able to help with the decorating . . ."

"Now you listen here," Dad shouted. "I'm sick and tired of hearing about your blasted party!"

I stepped back, almost tripping into the fire. I wasn't used to Dad shouting at me.

His voice softened. "Greg, it's only Tuesday — well,

Wednesday morning. What would be wrong with one extra night out in the mountains?"

"But that wasn't the deal. And I know you. Once you get up to Sky Lake, it will be even harder to get you back to Calgary."

He looked at me, his eyes pleading. "Neither Holly nor you will probably ever be on another trail ride again. It seems such a shame to come all the way out here and not spend a night or two at Sky Lake. It's so beautiful, you'd never forget it —"

"See! Now, you're saying a night *or two*!" I sat down on a stump and folded my arms. "Why do you guys get to decide everything? How come I don't have a say?" I was yelling again. If only I could calm myself down and reason with them, maybe they'd see things my way. Yelling wasn't doing any good. I took a deep breath.

But then Michael started in on me. "Greg, you're lucky to be out here in the mountains. Lots of people pay big bucks to go trail riding, and you get to be out here for free —"

"Oh, shut up."

Michael's eyes widened and his nostrils flared. "If you'd quit thinking about yourself all the time," he said, "and start thinking about others . . ."

"Like who?"

"Like Holly. She'd love to spend time in some high country."

"*I* don't need to think about Holly." The words rushed out and I was powerless to stop them. "*You* do enough thinking about her for all of us combined!"

Michael's face twisted. He threw himself against me, pushing me off the stump. My head hit the ground hard, but it was my brother, not me, that moaned. Then he disappeared into the darkness.

This was ridiculous, I thought. Now we'd all taken a turn getting mad and running off into the bushes. First me, then Holly, now Michael. One a day. Maybe it would be Dad's turn tomorrow. I picked myself up off the ground, checking the back of my head for cuts. Wow, that kid was strong.

Who would be the one to run after Michael? I wondered. Dad or Holly?

Fifteen

For a moment Holly stared into the fire, then, without even glancing at me, sighed and strode off in the direction that Michael had gone.

Dad was glaring at me. I was glad when he turned his gaze back to the fire. "Greg, why are you so frantic to get home? What is it you really want?"

"You know why."

"But what is there about any party that could be so important?"

I shrugged my shoulders, annoyed, because I wasn't sure anymore. "Maybe I just need to get away from all of you." I stared into the glowing coals of the fire. "What I want is to go home. And what you want is to stay out here. So who should have his way?"

"Do you know what I really want?"

I didn't answer.

He spoke slowly. "Greg, do you know what I want more than anything in the world?"

"Probably to live out here in the mountains with the horses all summer."

"Wrong." He cupped his face with his hands. "What I want more than anything in the whole world is for my two sons to get along."

"I'm afraid you'll have to wait a long time for that," I said in my most sarcastic voice.

"I'm afraid too." He knotted his fingers. "Sometimes I'm really afraid."

There was nothing I could say. I stared into the fading fire, avoiding his eyes, listening to the crack and sizzle of glowing coals. In the distance I could hear the muted voices of Holly and Michael, and ached to know what they were saying.

Dad and I sat there without talking for a long time.

"Michael lied and that's why Patches got away." My voice sounded loud in the silence. "That horse escaped because Michael lied to you. And you covered for him all this time."

"He told you."

"Yeah. You've never let *me* get away with lying! Why couldn't you just let everybody know what really happened?"

Dad raised his head. "Ha, you're one to talk! You sure didn't come out and tell us right away about catching Patches and losing him again up there, did you?"

"We didn't tell any lies — we said he got away from us. But last week Patches escaped just because Michael told you a deliberate lie. You've always taught us not to lie. How come you covered for him?"

"He already felt bad enough," Dad said. "I know I should have told the whole story — the whole truth. But Michael felt so terrible —"

"Michael, Michael. Everything is Michael. What about me?"

Dad's eyes widened. "That's funny. I've always worried that I try to please you the most, do what you want, care too much about what you think . . ."

Suddenly the conversation had become too heavy for me. I had to get us off this topic, and the sooner the better. I looked back to the fire and scratched at my dirty itchy hair. "Dad, just think of how good a nice hot shower would feel."

"You can wash your hair and have a bath tomorrow morning," my father said. "I'll start the water heating for you as soon as I wake up, and you can wash yourself in the tent while we're cooking breakfast."

"Don't you ever long for a real bath and your comfortable bed? And don't you miss Mom?"

"Of course! But when I get home I wish I were out here. I guess a person can't have everything in any one place. I just wish your mom wanted to share this with me."

I thought of myself lying on the moss, staring up at the sky with trees circled above me. And from nowhere came the sound of city traffic and the loud raucous laughter of my friends. I thought of the elk watching us, her eyes alive, her body poised and supple . . .

"Greg, you know what really feels great? Taking a sponge bath in the ice-cold river. Sounds crazy. But it's sure invigorating. If you can do without the hot water, you could head for the privacy of some willows down by the riverbank. It really wakes a guy up, that's for sure."

"I'm going to bed." I yawned.

"You must be very tired," Dad said.

"Yeah, you gotta be tough to be a cowboy."

But I couldn't sleep. I heard Holly come back to the fire and chat with Dad, small awkward talk as though she didn't know what to say. A few minutes later, Michael's voice asked, "Are we packing up to the lake tomorrow?"

Dad answered slowly. "Let's decide in the morning. I think we've all had enough for one day."

It was almost 3 a.m. When Holly came into the tent, I closed my eyes, pretending to be asleep. She climbed into her sleeping bag, then I could hear her moving restlessly.

Soon Dad came to bed. It must have been almost half an hour later when Michael crept into the tent. Had Michael dared to tell Holly how he felt? How would she react? Had he told her that Patches got away because he'd lied to Dad? Would it work? Would it make her like him even more?

I lay awake for a long time, trying to sleep, wishing for things to be the way they'd been only a few days before, longing to be back home where life had been much less complicated. Listening to the shallow breathing, I could tell that everyone else was still awake, too. Finally, I dozed off, but it was a restless sleep, full of swirling dreams.

I awoke before dawn to the sound of rain beating against the tent. Every muscle, every bone, every tendon hurt. Sighing, I adjusted my freezing aching bones on the thin foam mat, working around a tree root that seemed determined to poke through the middle of my back.

How many hours had we been riding yesterday? We had left camp before ten in the morning and got back after midnight. That made more than fourteen hours minus about three hours for eating lunch, arguing, stopping and trying to catch Patches. Eleven hours. Obscene. No city kid should have to spend eleven hours in a saddle.

I rolled over, trying to get back to sleep. In a minute the rain would stop and with any luck we could get going early and just ride up to catch Patches. Maybe they'd even go up there without me and I could stay down here for the day. . . . But the rain didn't quit. Somehow I drifted off to sleep.

When I awoke again, rain was still beating against the canvas. Through the tent shone gray morning light. My breath puffed white clouds into the icy air.

Dad was awake. Lifting his hand from the sleeping bag, he waved a silent hello. I almost laughed at how funny he looked with a wool toque pulled down to his eyes. He slid out of his sleeping bag, put on his slicker, traded the toque for his cowboy hat, laced his boots, then headed out into the rain. The horses whinnied the moment he lifted the tent flap.

Holding my breath, I listened, hoping that he'd rush right back to tell us Patches was standing out by our horses. But he didn't.

Might as well get up too, I decided. One good thing about sleeping with all your clothes on, you didn't have to waste time getting dressed. And when it was so cold that you even slept in your jacket, you were really ready to go.

July! This was supposed to be summer. It was probably hot and sunny in Calgary. I thought of Amanda in tight shorts with her slender suntanned legs and soft leather sandals. I looked at Holly. Just a bit of messy hair and one eye, scrunched in sleep, showed above her dirty old blue ski jacket at the edge of her sleeping bag. Real glamorous.

Had Michael dared to tell her how he felt? And if he had, what happened next? I tried to imagine Holly all mushy like Amanda or Janice, or especially like Linda who had chased me so relentlessly the year before. I almost laughed out loud. Somehow it didn't seem possible. It was hard even to imagine Holly kissing a guy. She seemed so independent, like a sister instead of a girlfriend.

She'd probably grow up to be an old maid like Aunt Eleanor. An old-maid schoolteacher with hair permed into little rolls along her head and . . . I almost laughed again. No, that wasn't Holly, either. Michael was right. There was definitely something special about her. Maybe she would suit him. Anyway, for a first girlfriend, it was probably good he didn't pick one who was too glamorous.

From outside the tent came the snap, snap of little branches. That meant Dad was gathering witch's hair, the long black and gray strands that hung from spruce branches. He always loved to tell us that it burned like gasoline, even in the wettest of weather.

I pulled my weary bones from the sleeping bag, wriggled into my rain slicker and staggered outside.

Dad had set the dishpans over the fire grate so he could start a fire without the rain putting it out. A heap of witch's hair burned as Dad fed bigger and bigger twigs into the growing yellow flame.

I looked around. Nope, no sign of Patches. I sat on a rain-soaked log, shaking with cold, until Dad got the fire going and we could huddle beside it to soak up a little warmth. The rain became lighter. Dad pointed to the big pan over the fire. "That can be bathwater," he said. "If you want it." Raindrops hissed as they hit the heated rocks around the pan.

"Sure." I didn't dare bring up the subject of today's agenda.

Seven o'clock. It was hard to believe I was awake before Michael. I wondered when that had ever happened before and could not remember a single time. I felt pleased with myself. But my gloating didn't last long. From the tent emerged a tousled head of hair, attached to a tall body in a yellow slicker.

Michael arranged his mouth into a groggy smile and said hi to me. At least he didn't seem angry about what I had said last night. Maybe it had been good to pull it out into the open so that he could talk to Holly about how he felt.

Michael headed for the pack-box cupboards, walking smoothly as though he had not ridden at all the day before.

Dad pointed to dark gray clouds churning in the west. "It's going to set in for some heavy rain. It's awful to pack everything up when it's raining," Dad said. "And a wet tent is a lot heavier."

"So we can just head up there for the day?" I asked.

Dad sighed. "What if we just relax this morning and hope the weather clears by noon? Who knows, Patches might still come wandering down."

"If he did appear in camp this morning," I said as pleasantly as possible, "could we just pack up this afternoon and go home?"

"Greg," Dad said quietly, looking at me with level unyielding eyes, "there will be other parties, you know. Could there be something out here you're afraid to face?"

I sputtered, ready to start yelling again. But Dad lifted his hands as if surrendering. "Don't worry, we'll go home as soon as possible. I'm tired of arguing with you." He put another few pieces of wood into the fire. "But how about just relaxing here for the morning?"

The way my body felt, I didn't mind the idea at all. No riding. A couple of more hours of sleep. A whole morning with absolutely nothing to do. I nodded. It felt like a truce. Really peaceful.

Dad looked pleased and I could see Michael's face relax, too. Funny, he didn't even seem mad at me this morning. Maybe there'd be some chance to get him on his own somewhere and find out how his talk with Holly had gone last night. It was great to think of getting back to sleep, of giving my body a chance to heal. I stretched. The city could wait one more day.

Michael led Lightning and Duke to the meadow to graze. Dad and I followed with the other horses. They were all soaked, dark and steamy, but I realized how good they must feel to have their muddy sweaty coats washed by the rain. Maybe this morning I *should* bathe my dirty body and wash my greasy hair.

The minute we got the horses to the meadow, they yanked at their halter ropes, pulling enthusiastically at the wet grass, swishing their tails with pleasure. Life was simple for a horse. Eat and sleep, and work if you had to. No worries. No mixed-up emotions.

Michael hobbled Lightning, glancing sideways at me, but I didn't say anything. A horse didn't belong in camp, and that was all there was to it.

Sixteen

By the time we trudged back to the campsite, rain was pouring so hard again we could hardly see the hills across the valley. Holly emerged from the tent looking tired and groggy. She peered around the meadow, no doubt searching for any sign of her pinto.

None of us talked much while we made breakfast and then stood eating, huddled under the tarp to keep dry. When Michael finished devouring four eggs, a dozen pancakes and a heap of bacon, he looked in the pack boxes. "Only two oranges left! Half for each of us and that's it!"

"I'd sacrifice my share for two guys who found my horse," Holly said. She looked at Dad, her chin jutting out. "Well, at least they found him. At least we know where to look for him now."

Dad nodded. "Okay. I'll give up my half, too. That leaves a whole orange for each of them."

Michael raised his hands to the sky and, with rain

running down the elbows of his slicker, said, "'The quality of mercy is not strained. It droppeth as the gentle rain from heaven.'" Then, grinning, he tossed me one of the oranges.

I figured I could put up with some Shakespeare for the sake of an orange, so I laughed and started to peel it eagerly, assuming he would eat his right away too. Michael surprised me, though. He looked longingly at his orange, but put it in his slicker pocket. I ate mine in a hurry, then washed the dishes. My hands felt good in the warm water.

When we finished the dishes, a sharp wind was rattling the tent and rain was striking us like icy needles. We ran for shelter, then sat in our sleeping bags, shivering and chatting. Holly and Dad started talking about university courses. Sure enough, she wanted to be a teacher. Michael pulled a book from his duffel bag and disappeared into his own private world.

"Wake me tomorrow morning," I said, snuggling deep into my sleeping bag.

There was something strangely cozy about soft gray light, the musty smell of wet canvas and the sound of heavy rain. Within minutes I was asleep.

I awoke with crusty teeth and a thick sour taste in my mouth. That was my reward for sleeping immediately after a big breakfast of bacon, eggs and pancakes. The rain had eased somewhat, but everyone was still asleep.

What had happened between Michael and Holly last night? I felt unraveled by all of this. Why did I care what had gone on between my brother and a girl? It was absolutely none of my business.

Might as well sleep some more. But I kept thinking about a little girl climbing on a bus with her pockets full of felt pens. Finally I decided to take a walk.

When I emerged from the tent, water cascaded off the canvas flap onto my hat brim. I tipped my head forward and the water poured in front of my face like a miniature waterfall. Down the muddy slope I headed, toward the horses, my slicker wrapping around my boots. And then I noticed a tiny bird on Smoky's back, a bird smaller than a child's fist, sitting relaxed, enjoying his ride on the enormous slippery-wet horse.

Two more tiny birds hopped through the grass around the horses' feet, then one of them jumped effortlessly onto Duke's back and sat watching me. Duke kept grazing.

The bird hopped off Duke's back as I approached, but didn't go far. I patted the horse's wet neck. "You didn't mind that little bird at all, did you, Duke?" I said. "Why can't Michael and I be like you guys? Two totally different species, but so relaxed together."

I laughed. "Look what's happened to me, Duke. Standing in the rain talking to a horse." Duke turned his head and I realized he was enjoying my touch, leaning against my hand to get more pressure. "I'm supposed to love my brother even when I don't like him," I said. "If only I could figure out how. It isn't much fun being at war."

I headed toward the river. It was much higher than before, fast and dirty, swollen from rain draining off the mountains. I walked past the place where Holly and I had talked that first night when I had stomped off in a huff because of Michael messing up the pack boxes.

That seemed so long ago. Sunday night. This was Wednesday. Ages ago, it seemed.

The rain had changed to a light drizzle. I walked faster. The path along the river was greasy with mud, so I headed for the meadow. Long wet grass swished at my boots and slicker. Glimpsing a movement in the trees, I stopped just as three white-tailed deer bounded up the riverbank and disappeared into the forest.

On I walked, surprised at how good it felt to be alone in such a fresh-smelling green world. Even my sore muscles and bones felt a little better with the exercise. By the time I started back to camp, the rain had stopped completely and the sky was showing some blue patches. The world looked clean and brand-new.

Everybody was up, poking around the pack boxes.

"Steak and lobster for lunch," Michael called as I came over the hill into camp, tripping on my long raincoat, sliding in the mud.

Holly grinned at me. "Yeah, disguised as canned beans and chicken noodle soup." But then she smiled at Michael too. I swallowed hard.

While we were eating our lunch, the clouds drifted away and the sun started to work its magic. Within half an hour, the air had warmed up several degrees.

"In a couple of hours the tent will be bone-dry," Dad said. "If anybody wants to wash their hair or bathe, better do it here. Sky Lake's too cold."

I took off my hat and stared across the valley, feeling desperate to escape. The sun heated my oily hair. Soon I was hot in my jacket, so I peeled it off and walked around in shirtsleeves, gathering dishes to throw into the dishpan.

Watching Michael put food and dishes into the cupboards, still keeping things the way I'd organized them, I wondered why he should have to change for my sake.

But if Michael were allowed to be himself, then I'd have to accept things that bugged me. So *I* would have to change. It didn't seem possible for us to coexist without one of us changing. There's the rub, as Hamlet would have said. I smiled. If only Michael knew that I was quoting Shakespeare to myself.

Holly climbed the riverbank carrying two pails full of water and poured them into the big pan over the fire. "Okay, guys, as soon as this water gets hot, the tent is off-limits. Bath time for this dirty old lady."

"I think I'll try the river," I said. "Nothing like blue sky, sunshine and mountains for bathroom decor."

She peered at me from under her eyebrows. "You're getting brave. The river's pretty cold."

"Maybe I'll get pneumonia and we'll *have* to go back to Calgary tonight." I flinched as I said that. It was my fault we weren't heading back today. There was no use blaming Michael.

"You'll have to work fast if you're going to get pneumonia by tonight."

"I always work fast," I replied, trying to keep the conversation light. Holly looked away, her cheeks red. Michael was watching me.

I went into the tent to find a towel, washcloth and clean clothes in my duffel bag.

"Take a garbage bag to stand on," Dad said.

That didn't seem necessary, but I decided not to argue. Garbage bag and towel over one arm, clean clothes over the other, I headed down the bank. "Make sure you go downstream, not upstream," Michael called. "We have to drink this water."

"Very funny."

"And watch out for bears," Dad said. "You've heard of bare naked . . ."

I groaned and headed toward the willows where I soon found a sheltered place beside the river. The bank wasn't very level, but it would do. I draped my clean clothes over the bushes.

Though I was sweating from my walk through the tangled willows, the idea of stripping made me shiver. Better get it over with as quickly as possible.

I peeled off my shirt and jeans, feeling foolish and vulnerable. Off with the socks. Mud tickled the soles of my bare feet. I glanced around to be sure no one was watching. Finally, off with the underwear.

Bending to dip the washcloth in the river, I almost slid in. Maybe I should have looked for a level spot.

The water felt freezing cold as I wet the soap and lathered the cloth against my skin. I rinsed myself by dipping the washcloth again and again into the river. Goose bumps rose on my tight skin, but I couldn't help smiling. It really did feel good on such a warm afternoon. Still, I couldn't make myself put my head in that icy river, so my hair would have to wait until I heated water back at camp.

I stood staring at the mountains, listening to the birds singing. Mud squished between my toes, soft and cool like margarine just out of the fridge. I put one foot in the river, felt it burn with the coldness of the water, watched the force of the current wash the mud off instantly.

I pulled my clean foot from the river and dipped the other one in. But then mud squished between the toes of my clean foot. I spread out the big black garbage bag, stood on it and dipped my feet again, one at a time. Standing on the plastic, they stayed clean. "Thanks, Dad," I said out loud.

Time to put on my clothes.

But first I lifted my hands to the sky and took a deep breath. It would feel great to holler. If only the tent weren't so close, I'd shout at the top of my lungs. Never in my life had I been able to do that, and somehow it would be just right out here to stand naked, yelling at the mountains. I smiled to myself, thinking of how fast three people would come running down the bank if I let out even a little holler.

Almost reluctantly I reached for my clothes. But just then I heard rustling in the bushes beside me. A bear? I spun around, lost my balance on the slippery plastic garbage bag and slid, feet first, right into the river.

Instantly the current pulled me downstream, frigid water paralyzing the muscles I needed for breathing. My frozen useless body hurtled past the blurry banks. I couldn't scream. I couldn't fight. Frantically I gasped for air.

Just before a corner, the river sucked my head under. This was it. I was going to drown. In terror I tried to close my throat against the overwhelming pressure of water. I was going to die!

But suddenly my body hit something solid. Struggling for my last molecules of air, I found the sky again. The river had swung me against the bank.

Up the slippery edge I crawled, then lay in the mud, gasping, coughing, shaking, but alive.

Finally I sat up, trying to calm my quivering muscles, still choking and coughing out water. My bones ached from coldness. I had to get back to my clothes. But what if a bear had been in those bushes? I couldn't go back there alone. Every year in the mountains, people were killed by bears, and I certainly didn't want to join the list.

On the other hand, if I yelled for help, Holly would come running with Dad and Michael, and I was hardly in a condition to receive female visitors.

I had no choice. I had to go back for my clothes. But something had been moving in those bushes. I thought of being found, dead and naked, mauled by a bear. It seemed much worse than being found mauled and dead with clothes on. At least there would be some dignity to that.

Shuddering, I looked away from the river. I could have been found naked and drowned.

Somehow I gathered the nerve to head upstream. Shaking, I scrambled along the bank, terrified to even glance at the churning river.

Ouch. My bare foot landed on a broken willow stem sticking out of the mud. I waited for the pain to subside, then limped on. Branches scratched my skin. I was finding out that clothes were meant for more than warmth and looks.

Near my bathing place, I stood listening, my heart thumping. My imagination conjured up a ferocious bear with gigantic teeth and claws.

On I tramped, not daring to yell for help. Just a few

more minutes and I'd be at the place where I had fallen in. I could hardly breathe as I walked closer and closer to where the terrible bear must be . . .

It turned out to be a great nonevent. Just bushes, blue sky and innocent birds chirping. Whatever had made the noise must have moved on. But my once-clean body was covered with mud, twigs and leaves. I'd have to bathe all over again before I could get dressed. I checked out my scratches and cuts, gathering courage, then trembling, picked up the washcloth and bent cautiously toward the ice-cold swollen river.

Finally clean and clothed, I headed up the bank, exhausted. Only Holly was in camp. Good thing I hadn't yelled for help. She had finished bathing, changed clothes and was pouring hot water into a plastic bucket. "Just my hair left," she said, smiling. Then she noticed my wet head. "Greg, did you wash your hair in that freezing river?"

"More than that," I said. By the time I finished telling Holly about my near-drowning, her pan of water was cold. While the water was heating again over the fire, we talked. I hadn't realized that she had never really said anything about her fall in the river on Sunday. But now she told me that when the current had been pulling her under, she, too, had thought she would die.

"Mom and Dad must never know that I fell in the river," she said. "Never."

When the water was hot again, Holly dunked her head into the pail and lathered her hair with shampoo. "Could you help me rinse?" she asked.

I filled the other pail, then slowly poured warm water over her scalp. It seemed such a close personal thing to do for a girl. I watched steam rise off her head and water run down her face. A brand-new feeling fluttered through my chest. Was it tenderness? Whatever it was, it terrified me.

Holly dumped out the dirty water. "Mud!" she said.

Again I poured rinse water over her bowed head. Then she wrapped an old blue towel around her hair and flipped her head back so the towel fell into place like a headdress.

Helpless and blind, she groped for her glasses. When she put them on, her eyes came to life again. Despite those funny old-fashioned frames, she looked like some kind of princess, with her head tilted back slightly and the blue towel framing her face. Holly, you certainly aren't ugly, I thought.

I let my breath out. Come on, Kepler, I told myself, this is ridiculous. You've been away from a real girl so long that anything would look good. And how come you only started really noticing Holly when you found out that your brother liked her?

Or maybe it was because we'd both nearly drowned. Nothing like common experiences to cement a relationship!

Grabbing two empty pails I headed for the river. Time to wash *my* hair. In *warm* water. Maybe it would clear my head at the same time.

Seventeen

As I set the pan full of water over the fire, smoke stung my eyes and choked my lungs. "Stupid smoke," I sputtered.

"Don't worry," Holly said, "it will all be worth it. A person feels different with clean hair. Whenever I get cranky, my Dad always teases me that I'd better go wash my hair."

I laughed but it came out squeaky. This was the first time I'd felt awkward around any girl. Where was Dad? And Michael, where had he gone? I thought again of Michael and Holly talking by the river the night before. Here was my chance to ask her what happened, but now I wasn't even sure I wanted to know.

Easing my sore body onto a stump, I sat waiting for the water to heat. A cool wind had blown in. I got up to put on my jacket, then looked at my watch. Three o'clock. To think that just twenty-four hours ago Michael and I had been riding up the mountain to find Patches.

Holly sat on another stump, took the towel off her head and started pulling a comb through her thick dark hair. She looked out toward the meadow again. "I still can't get over that you guys managed to catch him," she said.

"It was just like what you suggested a couple of days ago," I told her. "We figured it out step by step, like solving a math problem."

"Well, you earn full marks." She still hadn't taken her eyes off the meadow.

My stomach tightened.

"Just another few hours and I'll have my old horse back!" She smiled. "I'm sure looking forward to seeing Sky Lake. My dad says it's one of the most beautiful spots on earth, and he's traveled to a lot of different countries."

"It's just a lake, isn't it?" Why did I feel so crabby all of a sudden? Maybe I did need my hair washed. Why was the water taking so long to heat? I put some more wood on the fire, and coughed again when the smoke swung into my face.

"People should go out of their way to make good memories," Holly said softly. "When you're old you'll forget what you had for breakfast that day, but you'll remember things that happened years before."

She gazed across the valley. "It's funny. The only reason Mom and Dad allowed me out here was because I had to catch Patches, and then I almost wasn't even needed for that."

"I'm glad you came along." I couldn't believe I'd said such a dumb thing.

She grinned. "I'm glad you're here, too."

My heart was pounding. Why did I feel so awkward? I had used so many lines on glamorous girls, rolled glib words off my tongue like oil, silky, without any effort. No fear involved. And here was a girl that wasn't the least bit glamorous and I was feeling like a foolish pup.

I thought I had problems with Michael! Now things were really getting complicated. What was I going to do about Holly and me — and Michael? I rubbed the back of my neck.

"You're just aching to head home, aren't you?" She looked wistfully toward the mountaintops.

"Well, I have this party . . ."

"There'll be other parties."

Dad had used the same words a few hours before. There was silence again, then she spoke slowly. "Greg, I need to talk to you about something."

I didn't dare answer.

"It's about Michael. You probably know what it is." She fidgeted with the towel that was draped over her shoulder, twisting the raveled edge. "He, uh, told me that he, well, you know."

I swallowed hard. Why did she need to talk to *me* about it?

She stared at the ground. "Michael is so interesting and such a character. I love when he comes with your Dad to our place so we can ride together and talk. In fact, Michael is one of my best friends. Maybe my very best friend. I guess that's the scary part."

She laughed nervously. "I've seen too many great friendships ruined by, well, you know what I mean. The problem is to figure out how to keep it as just friendship. I don't want to hurt him, and I want to keep him as a friend. . . ."

She wasn't in love with him. Poor Michael. She didn't want him. I felt guilty for being so relieved. "Holly, you're sure different from other girls." I hadn't meant to say that. Shut up, I told myself.

She laughed. "Yeah, I'm different all right."

Just then I saw Dad heading back along the creek with a towel hanging around his neck and his arms full of dirty clothes. Michael was strolling beside him, talking, his yellow-cover wildflower book in one hand, his camera in the other.

"Well," Dad said as they walked into camp, "no sign of Patches. And the tent's dry. Are you guys ready to pack up?" He watched for my reaction — like Michael said he always did.

I shrugged, and thought of my friends laughing, talking, getting things ready. Without me.

Then I glanced at Holly and nodded. She was beaming. Suddenly I felt really good. And I hadn't even washed my hair yet.

Dad watched as I grabbed a towel and lifted the basin of hot water from the fire. "So, Greg, how did the river bath go?" he asked.

"Remember you told me that bathing by the river really wakes a person up?"

He nodded, puzzled.

"Well, I'd have to agree with you." As I told Dad and Michael what had happened, they both sat listening with wide worried eyes. They really did care about me!

Dad helped me pour water into the plastic pail, and I dunked my head in, my warm wet hair steaming in the cold air. My head felt hot and cold, the same delicious sharp contrast as in sweet and sour Chinese food.

Dad handed me the shampoo bottle then walked towards the cupboards. When I ducked my lathered head into the pail, I was amazed at how dirty the water became. "More mud than you, Holly Wilson," I said.

She smirked. "I'll help you rinse."

I knelt as she poured the water over my head. It took a couple of rinses before the water stayed clear.

"Feels better to rinse your hair in warm water than in the river, eh, Greg?" Dad said, his voice close by again. "Sure good that river didn't get you."

I didn't answer because of the lump in my throat, but the way Dad was looking at me, I knew he didn't expect an answer. He laid his hand on my shoulder. It was the first time I could remember him doing that to me.

We all stood there awkward and silent. "Well, gang," Dad said at last, "let's get the show on the road. Patches is waiting." Within a few minutes the tent was down. I organized the boxes. It was easy with so little food left.

Everyone seemed in a better mood. Michael and Dad joked while they loaded the packhorses. Holly whistled as she saddled our riding horses. Before five o'clock we were ready to go. I lowered my aching backside onto the hard leather saddle and sighed.

I thought of offering to take Smoky so Holly wouldn't have to lead a packhorse, but wondered what Michael would think, so I said nothing.

We came to the river. I glanced down, shivered, and forced my eyes to focus on the mountains as Duke pushed his way through the swirling water. Then I looked back and watched Holly crossing, her face tight.

We headed into the thick spruce forest and started our climb, stopping often to give the horses a breather. The trail seemed so different without fog or darkness.

When we came to the fork, of course Michael and Dad insisted we had to take the high trail, the one that would lead us up along the ridge, the famous scenic branch of the trail that my brother and I hadn't taken the day before because of the fog. The climb became extremely steep. Then we rode around a corner and Holly let out a low whistle. "Good grief!"

I knew we were really in for something.

As Duke rounded the corner, I saw what Holly meant. "Good grief!" I said.

"That's a perfect name for it." Dad laughed. "Good Grief Hill." The path went almost straight up, wide with no grass, just dirt churned by countless hooves. Obviously lots of trail riders went up there. But how?

Dad slid off Muggs. "We don't ride up this one. We walk and lead the horses."

"You don't mean 'walk,'" Holly said. "You mean 'crawl.' What if Bud gets scared and rears? He'd drag me with him straight over that edge."

"I'll lead him for you," Dad said. "Here, Greg, you take Ginger. Muggs doesn't need leading."

Dad looped his reins around Mugg's saddle horn and let her go. Then he started up the sharp incline, pulling at Bud's halter rope. Sure enough, the crazy horse reared, his eyes rolling back, hooves pawing the air, but Dad kept him going and soon the horse was puffing so hard he didn't have enough energy left for any nonsense.

Muggs followed Dad all by herself, blowing hard,

her legs bent as though she were crawling. I knew I'd never again make fun of how ugly that mare looked. Holly went next with Smoky. Duke and Ginger followed me, clambering sensibly and carefully against the dangerous steepness.

Michael, Lightning and Lucky were behind us. I looked back and was surprised at how calmly Lightning was behaving. When we were halfway up the hill, Michael called, "Holly, Greg, look back." I looked and felt dizzy at the height and open space. Duke's reins and Ginger's halter rope in one hand, I grabbed hold of a bush at the side of the trail, to keep my balance.

Far across the valley were snow-capped mountains with patches of forest like green shag rugs along their sides. Far below, a silver river wound through the valley.

"Wow!" Holly said.

Michael laughed. "Wait till you see the view when we ride along the ridge!" He pointed. "That's our camp down there. That tiny speck at the base of the hill."

I shook my head. "How could we have come so far?"

"Amazing, isn't it." He was speaking softly.

Our eyes met, held for a moment, then we both looked back toward the valley.

"We *have* come a long way." There was a funny tone in his voice. I knew he meant more than I was willing to admit. So I laughed. He patted Lightning's sweaty neck.

When we reached the top of Good Grief Hill, we stood gasping for air. We could no longer see the view, because the tall thick forest closed everything in. I thought about home and wondered if city life would enclose me enough to make me forget all this.

Dad took Ginger back from me and we swung onto our horses. Again I wondered if I should offer to take Smoky to give Holly a break from leading a packhorse, but I didn't dare because Michael might think I was playing up to her.

The trail kept climbing through the forest. Holly turned to grin at me and my heart thumped.

She had said she needed to talk to me about Michael liking her. Why me? My chest felt as though it were full of butterflies. This was ridiculous. She just wanted me for a friend. She didn't want anybody falling for her. Besides, she wasn't my type. I winced just thinking of how Ken and the other guys would make fun of me if I ever started to go around with Holly Wilson.

I watched the way she sat on Bud, moving easily with him. Michael and Dad sat that way, too, moving with their horses. They never got stiff.

Drawing a deep breath, I commanded my muscles to relax. To my surprise, I did feel better, as though I were part of the rhythm of Duke's footsteps. I tried to relax even more, allowing my body to swing with his rocking motion. Another deep breath. The air tasted good.

Dad never took his eyes off the trail below us, even when we were climbing through the trees. When we reached the timberline, we could see down into Forbidden Valley again. Holly gazed across the valley, smiling. It was a pleasure to see anybody that happy. It would be a shame to go back in a hurry.

All around and above us was gray rock, here and there some short scruffy grass and a few small wildflowers. Then I saw it. A thick green mosslike mat, big as a pillow, its top almost completely covered with hundreds of tiny pink flowers. "What on earth. . . ?" I said.

"Moss pink." Michael stopped Lightning. "It's a big one."

"Incredible." Holly bent low over Bud's neck for a better look. "Moss pink?"

"Also called moss campion. *Silene acaulis*," he said almost reverently.

"I think that's the most beautiful thing I've ever seen," Holly said.

Dad smiled. "Good place for a break, then."

I nodded. We slid off the horses and sat on the rocks beside the enormous green-and-pink plant.

I touched it and was surprised. What looked like a thick green pillow of the softest moss was actually a mat of tiny crisp sharp projections, thousands of them, like stiff little bristles. Things could sure be different than they looked.

"Smell it," Michael said, and to my amazement I found myself obeying him, bending to smell the pink mat of flowers, which covered most of the green pillow. They had a sweet smell, almost like roses.

I inhaled more deeply. Last summer I'd given a dozen red roses to Linda. They had smelled great, like this. But Linda had started phoning me, writing notes in class, chasing me so much I had to start running.

I'd never given roses to anyone again. Funny thing, before the roses, Linda had been so cold to me. You never knew how things were going to turn out.

Holly was watching me. She bent to smell the moss pink, too.

"Touch the green part," Michael said.

She put her hand out to stroke it, then pulled back. "Sharp. It looks so soft. But it's sharp and prickly."

"Like some people," he said. "They might seem soft, but they're harder than you imagine." She glanced up. Their eyes met, and instead of looking away, Holly smiled at him, a gentle smile that spread across her face. Their faces were much too close, but neither moved back. Finally they both looked down at the moss pink.

Dad was standing by Muggs totally absorbed in tightening his cinch. Now Michael's hand was close to Holly's on the green of the moss campion. I wasn't jealous. Never felt jealous in my life over a girl. I could make any girl I chose fall for me like a ton of bricks. If I really tried I could get Holly too. But I didn't want her.

I glared at Holly. What had happened to her wonderful speech about not spoiling friendship with love? How come now she was falling for Michael like some dumb little twit? A pain twisted through my stomach. I looked back over the valley.

Holly stood up first. Michael was perched above the moss pink. When he tried to stand, his foot slipped and his leg slid from underneath him. Giggling, Holly reached out her hand. When she pulled him up I noticed that their hands stayed clasped much longer than they needed to.

What was wrong with Holly? What did she see in Michael?

"You ready to go?" Dad called. "It's not far now."

It might not be far, but I had lost interest in seeing Sky Lake.

Tomorrow night we'd be in Calgary. It had been only

four days since we'd left home. I sighed. After tomorrow I'd be back in control, enjoying my car and my
friends. And girls. Pretty girls. Not some thick girl with
thick glasses who didn't even know her own mind.

Eighteen

Finally we reached the top of the ridge and it was true. The whole world did lie below us. Without a word we dismounted our puffing animals and stood staring. All around were valleys and layer upon layer of blue and purple mountains, each one paler than the one in front of it. Three hundred and sixty degrees, all around us. And the river thin as a thread.

I felt like a tiny speck, insignificant, and yet strangely like the king of the universe. Tears came to my eyes. It was from the wind for sure. It was strong, flapping our jackets. Holly was standing between Michael and me, staring at the far horizon. Her eyes dampened, too.

I looked straight down the side of the narrow ridge and felt dizzy. What if one of us fell? There wouldn't be anything to break the fall.

Nobody said a word, not even Michael. I heard him take a deep breath. We all seemed so close, standing staring at the scene around and below us. Finally, still silent, we mounted our horses. On to Sky Lake.

Along the narrow rock ridge we rode, the wind pushing against our backs. I clung to my saddle horn, white-knuckled, grateful for such a surefooted sensible horse. Even Bud was walking carefully as though he knew he had no choice. Or maybe he was just tired.

I looked down and felt giddy. Everything seemed different up here, cleaner, almost scrubbed. Looking at the green grass and wildflowers, I couldn't believe there had been a full-fledged blizzard here just five days before. Snow up to the horses' knees, the man had said. Things sure could change in a hurry.

Michael and Holly weren't even looking at each other now as they rode along, Michael in front, Holly behind him. Maybe I had imagined things back there by the moss pink. We rode past more moss pinks, some small like saucers, some as large as dinner plates, but none as spectacular as that first one.

Maybe Holly had smiled at Michael that way just because she had been so thrilled with the moss pink and the beautiful mountains. And what was the big deal about her pulling him up and the way they had laughed together? When you're feeling happy you do fun things like that. Just good friends. That's what she wanted. I had probably imagined all the other stuff.

I could feel my muscles loosen and my forehead relax. Enjoy the scenery, I told myself. You can brag about this ride to your friends next week. Would they be interested? I wondered how much they really cared about me. Did it matter to them what I felt or thought? Or did they just care if I fit in?

Holly turned around and grinned at me. I grinned back at her, my heart thumping.

The path headed downward, very steep, the horses skidding over loose rock, and finally we joined the trail that Michael and I had ridden the day before.

Farther down we went, back into forest, then out of the trees, up a steep hill covered with short clumps of windswept grass. Barricade Mountain loomed over us, larger and larger as we neared the top of the hill. And suddenly there below was Sky Lake.

It looked so tiny. Sky Lake. Deep turquoise, shiny, almost round. The enormous mountain seemed to hold the little lake in its huge pebbly gray arms. To the right, small scruffy trees and short grass sheltered in a rock crevice. In front of the lake a few stunted trees stood as though painted on canvas. Thick snowbanks covered much of the gravel slope around the lake. Snowbanks in July! A ridge of shale rose to the right, with a narrow trail worn over the rocks. Michael pointed. "See, Greg, that's the trail you and I took yesterday down to the north valley."

"Looks a little different without the fog," I said.

We tied the horses to the tiny trees and scrambled down the bank, a thick layer of loose pebbles giving way under our feet, some tumbling and bouncing to the edge of the lake. The smell of cold water freshened the air.

As we approached, the color of the lake changed from turquoise to emerald-green. By the time we reached the shore, it was royal blue with black edges. The water was so clear we could see fish swimming.

The only sound was the hollow rattle of a few

pebbles still rolling from our footsteps. Then all was quiet. We stood staring as breezes quivered along the surface of the lake.

"It's so little." That was a dumb thing to say. But no one laughed at me.

"It's not really as small as it looks." Dad spoke slowly. "It would take you almost half an hour to walk around it. It seems small because Barricade Mountain is so huge.

"Well, we'd better go unpack these horses and set up camp," Dad said. "Then maybe we can come back here and catch some fish for supper. We could have our own little party tonight. Fresh fish and —" he laughed " — Kool-Aid." He smiled at me. "And tomorrow, at last, Greg, you can go home."

I nodded, not knowing what to say. Nobody had mentioned Patches, but I knew that everyone had been looking around for him all the time. Maybe he'd be in camp. We trudged back to the horses.

"I think I'll just walk," I said.

Heart pounding, lungs gasping the thin air, I led Duke to the top of the steep hill, then back down into the trees. It felt good to move my stiff sore legs.

Patches wasn't in camp. "He might be in one of the meadows around here," Dad said as he and Michael lifted the pack boxes off Smoky. But I could see that they were worried. I kept hearing the echo of my loud "Shut up!" and the sound of Patches running away in the dark.

Michael stared out at Barricade Mountain. His face was hardly swollen anymore. In fact, except for the faded yellow-and-purple ring around one eye, he looked almost normal. Good, I said to myself, let's keep it that way.

Michael had wanted so desperately to bring Holly's horse back to her. Poor Michael. And the first girl he fell for didn't want him. I just wished I didn't feel so relieved.

As soon as the horses were unpacked and unsaddled, we led them through the trees to the closest meadow. Dad was in front with Muggs and Lucky. At the edge of the clearing he stopped. "Hallelujah!" he shouted, pointing at the ground. We all gathered to see what he had found.

I never dreamed I could feel so happy to see a pile of fresh horse manure. Patches was somewhere nearby!

We forgot all about the idea of catching fish for supper. It was after seven and everyone was starved, but as soon as we hobbled the horses, we started walking around, searching the surrounding forest. "Patches! Patches!" yelled Holly.

"Will he come when you call?" I asked her.

"No." She laughed. "Never. But it makes me feel like I'm doing something."

At first we searched eagerly, assuming we'd find him right away. But as we combed the woods, over and over, finding another couple of fresh droppings but no horse, we became quieter and quieter.

"He must be around here somewhere," Michael said.

"My crazy old horse." Holly shook her head. "He's probably enjoying his freedom so much he's decided to stay hidden forever."

"Tell you what," Dad said. "Let's go make supper.

He'll probably come to visit our horses as soon as we leave."

I noticed that Michael had hobbled Lightning again. Before we left the meadow, my brother strolled over to his horse, gave him a hug, then headed for camp, his head bent.

As we started making supper, Lightning came shuffling into camp. "See?" Michael said. "It doesn't help to hobble him. He's still a kitchen rat." He unhobbled the horse, said, "Sorry, fellow," and started to lead him toward the trees.

"Where are you going?" I asked.

"To tie him up." He leaned his head against Lightning's neck and stroked him. "It's the only way to keep him out of the camp kitchen."

"Well, uh, maybe every well-equipped camp needs a kitchen rat," I said.

Michael stared at me, his mouth open.

I shrugged. "You know, to eat carrot peelings, keep the cook company . . ."

A smile spread across his face. His eyes lit up. "I could make sure he doesn't drink any dishwater."

"And he's not allowed in my sleeping bag," I said. "We need a few rules, you know." Then everyone was laughing, including me.

After supper, we checked the meadow. Still no sign of Patches. We did the dishes and hiked to the meadow again. Lightning sauntered behind us. A wind was blowing in, and the air seemed much cooler. "We'd better get the tent up," Dad said, "in case it starts raining."

Oh, no, I thought. I was so tired of rain. Funny thing, in the city I hardly noticed the weather. Out here it was so important.

As soon as we had the tent set up and the camp organized, Michael went over to his saddlebags, dug around and pulled out an orange. My eyebrows lifted. The last orange. "Catch, Greg."

I caught it, puzzled.

He smiled. "It's yours."

"But, I had mine. This morning."

"Well, this one can be yours, too."

"I can't take your orange."

"Take it."

"But it was my horse that squished most of our oranges. So I shouldn't have the last one."

"Listen to him, you guys." Holly cupped her ear with one hand. "*My* horse. We're going to make a cowboy out of him yet."

We laughed, drunk with the thin air.

I said, "Now, about this orange . . ." Handing it back to Michael, I met his eyes. "I, uh, just can't eat it."

He grinned. "Take advantage of me. It doesn't happen very often."

I divided his orange into four, and we all shared it, the sticky juice running down our fingers, over our lips. It tasted sweet as sugar. "This is a celebration party," Michael said.

My forehead wrinkled. "We haven't caught the horse yet. Why would we be celebrating?"

"You didn't drown in the river," he said quietly. I swallowed.

Together we sawed and chopped wood for breakfast.

My arms ached from sawing, but somehow that felt good too. While we were stacking the wood, Michael said, "Do you know that wood warms you three times?"

Holly looked up. "Three times?"

"Once when you cut it, once when you carry it and once when you burn it."

We groaned.

Soon the wind was really howling, and heavy clouds moved in over the top of Barricade Mountain.

Holly frowned. "Won't Patches head down into one of the valleys if there's a storm?"

"No," Dad said, "he'll probably be more nervous and want to stay near our horses for comfort. Don't worry, if we don't catch him tonight, for sure we'll get him tomorrow morning." He looked at me. "And then we'll head home."

As he spoke, the wind eased up and suddenly water poured from the sky. We rushed to cover the firewood with a tarp before running to the tent.

I was surprised how peaceful it felt inside the tent with rain beating against the canvas and hazy evening light shining through. We started telling silly jokes, the dumb ones little kids love. Normally the jokes wouldn't be funny, but that night everything seemed hilarious.

"How can you tell if there's an elephant in your shower?" I asked.

Nobody knew.

"You can smell peanuts on his breath." They moaned, and I laughed until my sides hurt, rolling around on my sleeping bag.

From down in the meadow a horse squealed.

For just a split second, we all froze. We stared at each

other, our eyes wide, then grabbed our slickers and hats to rush out into the rain, and through the mud to the edge of the clearing.

The squeal again. But it was just Smoky scolding Bud because he was grazing too close.

Back in the tent, Holly asked, "How do you fit five elephants in a sports car?"

We gave up.

"Two in the front seat and three in the back."

Again the squealing. We looked at each other. "Guess I'd better go and check again." Dad reached for his hat.

"I'll go," Michael said. He put his slicker and hat back on, then ducked out through the wet canvas flap.

For a few minutes we sat waiting, listening. But Michael didn't yell or come rushing into the tent, so obviously it hadn't been Patches. We started joking and laughing again.

Suddenly I wasn't laughing anymore. Along with the pounding of the rain, I was sure I had heard sniffing sounds at the back of the tent. Sniffing sounds. I could hardly breathe. The hair on my arms stood up.

"A bear," I whispered. Holly and Dad were sitting with their eyes frozen open, like me. More sniffing and then clumsy scratching against the canvas.

"The gun," Dad said. "It's out on my saddle."

Nineteen

Dad looked around frantically. "Michael!" he called.

The scratching stopped. Blood pounded in my ears. All three of us sat paralyzed, listening. Then something pushed against the tent wall, and we heard more sniffing. Our eyes widened. We wouldn't have a chance if a bear slashed through the canvas. There wasn't anything in the tent that could be used as a weapon.

"Michael!" Dad called once more. "Michael, can you hear me? Get the gun. There's a bear behind the tent."

The scratching and sniffing stopped again. A few seconds later Michael burst into the tent, water pouring off his slicker, laughing. "You guys sure fell for that one."

"Michael," Dad said quickly. "There's a bear at the back of the tent —"

"It was me."

"You?"

"Sure." My brother sniffed around and scratched his fingers against the canvas. It had been him all right. Dad and Holly burst out laughing.

"Michael," Holly said, "you are one crazy guy!" Her eyes were shining, open, admiring. My chest tightened.

"Well, we'd been joking about bears so much." Michael grinned. "So I just thought —"

"You never think," I said. "That's the problem. Scaring us to death . . ." Everybody stopped laughing and looked at me, their faces taut. And that made me feel worse.

"I was just trying to be funny," Michael said quietly.

"Well, scaring people isn't what I'd call funny. And what if Dad had his gun in here and shot at you? You're so stupid."

Holly twisted the edge of her jacket. "Greg, please . . ."

"Yeah, I know, I know. If I can't like him, I'm supposed to love him. Or something dumb like that." She glared at me and it felt as though the sun had burned out. I turned to Michael, fighting tears. "Love you? Like you? Care about you? What if I can't do any of those?"

Michael's shoulders sagged, his eyes suddenly wet. "Maybe you could . . ." He bent his head. "Maybe you could . . . *put up* with me?"

Suddenly I wanted more than anything in the world to throw my arms around him the way I had done on that hill after we caught Patches. And maybe if Dad and Holly hadn't been there I would have.

Instead I sat like a punctured balloon, the life gone

out of me. I thought of how much it must have hurt Michael when Holly told him last night that she just wanted to be friends with him. He had been trying hard today, trying to be brave and funny when he probably felt like crying. He hadn't needed me slicing at his guts.

"Sure is raining hard," Holly said.

Dad looked up. "Just wait a . . ."

" . . . minute," we all chimed in, then laughed awkwardly.

"If I could find another orange," I said, turning to Michael. "I'd give it to you."

He laughed, sniffing, wiping at his eyes. Holly smiled at me. I hadn't known a smile could make such a difference.

"By the way, Michael," Dad asked, "what were the horses squealing about?"

"Oh, Bud and Smoky were just fighting for the same little spot of lush green grass." Michael rubbed his hand against his wet cheeks. "Stupid horses." Then all of us were smiling again.

We went out and together brought the horses in from the meadow, led them to the lake for a drink, tied them to some trees for the night, then went to sleep, lulled by the steady beat of rain against the tent.

* * *

I awoke shivering. It was cold, so cold my breath formed thick white puffs. It wasn't raining anymore! I knew it must be very early. The sun shone low, casting a yellow glow inside the tent. I looked at my watch. Only five-thirty!

Birds sang all around the tent. I'd never heard birds

sing so enthusiastically. But then I'd never been awake so early on a sunny morning in the mountains.

This was Thursday. For sure we'd find the old guy today. And then, Dad had said, we could go home right away.

Suddenly I noticed patterns on the east wall of the tent. They were shadows from the sun shining through bushes and grass. I lay staring at the patterns. Tiny leaves, big leaves, long slender blades of grass, all silhouetted sharp and black against the yellow glow of the dirt-stained canvas. In a little while the sun would be higher, and the patterns would disappear.

Should I wake everybody so they could see the beautiful shadows? Michael and Dad had probably seen tent-wall art like that dozens of times. But Holly would love it. Naw, better let them sleep.

Quietly I slid out of my sleeping bag, laced on my boots and opened the flap of the tent. Immediately the horses whinnied, impatient to be out grazing.

White frost coated the grass, and a thick layer of ice covered the drinking water in the plastic pail. Blue sky. Not a cloud. I breathed in deeply, savoring the sweet smell of spruce, the smell of Christmas trees in July.

I wandered to the meadow. Empty. When I returned, the whole gang was up, the sun had moved higher, and the tent patterns were gone.

We led the horses to the meadow, then searched for almost half an hour, through the forest and down into the next clearing. Nothing. But there was fresh manure in among the trees. Patches had been there some time during the night.

By eight o'clock we had finished breakfast and had the horses saddled. Leaving Smoky, Lucky and Ginger tied to trees, we rode out. The plan was to search the forest and meadows a bit farther away and, if necessary, after lunch, head back down into the valleys.

"Maybe we should change partners," Dad said. "Greg, how about you and I riding together today?" I looked from Dad to Holly and back to Dad. I'd have killed for this chance a couple of days ago. Dad pulled up Muggs beside me, waiting for my answer.

If I rode with Dad, Michael would be with Holly. Knowing the way everybody ended up under Michael's spell sooner or later, I didn't want the two of them alone, especially out here. It seemed that things happened real fast out here away from the real world.

I shuffled my feet in the stirrups. "Aw, Holly and I are kinda used to riding together now."

"It's your choice," Dad said, looking sad. Michael looked even sadder. Suddenly I felt like saying I'd changed my mind, I'd love a chance to ride with my father. But Michael and Dad were already turning their horses into the forest.

Holly and I went in the other direction. She had made no comment, but I wondered what she was thinking. I found myself making small talk and felt annoyed, wishing for the peaceful feeling I'd had around her just a couple of days before. She seemed as relaxed as ever. The problem was me.

I cared about her, cared far too much. There, I had admitted it. To myself at least. That should have made me feel better. But it didn't. I felt like I was drowning again, being pulled under by fierce icy water.

"How come Patches is so hard to catch?" I asked her as we rode through a clearing full of little blue flowers.

"I don't know. He was always that way, sneaky and suspicious. The people who had him before us had to keep thinking of new ways to catch him — chasing him through smaller and smaller corrals, hiding a loop of string in a pail of oats, trying to grab his halter when they were on another horse, whatever. But the more they tricked him, the sneakier he got. So that's why they sold him. Real cheap too."

"How come you can catch him?"

"We sure couldn't at first," she said, pushing up her glasses. "But Jonathan and I spent so much time brushing him and talking to him. We quit being sneaky. We'd stand with his halter draped in full view over our arms when he came for his pail of oats, and we wouldn't even try to catch him. Gradually we could rub him with the halter and finally put it on him, but then we'd just feed him oats, brush him and let him go without riding him."

She grinned. "Eventually we could walk up to him anywhere even with no oats and his halter swinging from our hands. Nobody else had ever bothered to go through all that."

"What if all this chasing around makes it so you can't catch him?" I asked. "You know, how Madge Galleger said he was getting sneakier and sneakier —" I bent my head " — and how I scared him away."

"No." She smiled. "He wouldn't forget years of trusting somebody just because of what's happened in a few days. But I'm sure he's getting a taste for freedom. Funny, Jonathan always said Patches should have been born a wild horse, free to roam the mountains."

"You sure must miss him. Your brother."

"I guess it's one of the loneliest things in the world. To be an only child. Especially when you're not used to it." She pushed the hair away from her face and tried to smile.

Michael could have been riding with Holly all morning. She had said he was probably her best friend. What right did I have to come between them?

We met Michael and Dad in one of the clearings and rode with them back for lunch. As we neared our campsite, we heard the pounding of hooves galloping away. We hurried into camp. The ground was all scuffed up, and the horses we'd left behind were excited, but there was no sign of a pinto.

"How could he gallop dragging a halter rope?" Michael asked.

"He's smart," Holly said. "It wouldn't have taken him long to learn to run with his head to one side."

"The way he was galloping, he's probably far away by now," I said. "Let's leave the horses tied in camp and head down to the lake for lunch. He'll only come back if we leave."

"Good idea," said Dad. "We'll bring our rods and catch some fish for supper while we're at it."

Carrying lunch, fishing rods, bait box and net, we hiked up the windblown hill. "That would make quite a picture," Holly said. "The little sparkling lake and that huge gray mountain all around it. Looks like a turquoise jewel set in a thick silver bracelet. And that blue, blue sky."

"If you like blue sky," Dad said, "you'd better get your picture now. I bet this wind is going to blow something up pretty soon."

So Michael went back to camp for the camera and took a picture of us on the grassy hill with Sky Lake below. Then we climbed down the loose gravel bank and sat on the huge boulders by the lake, eating our lunch. When we had scraped the last morsel of tuna from the cans and devoured every crumb of the cookies, Holly headed back to camp to see if Patches had returned.

She was gone for quite a while and we were beginning to feel hopeful. But then she appeared at the crest of the hill shaking her head.

"What worries me," Michael said when she sat beside us again, "is that he seems to have gone north. What if he goes all the way back down to the Galleger's camp?"

I picked up a pebble and shook it in my hands. "But Madge told us they wouldn't be coming back until tomorrow night, so he wouldn't find anybody to visit. You'd think he'd eventually wander back up here again."

"He wouldn't go that far anyway," said Dad. "He'd want to stay near the horses he knows."

Michael picked up his rod. "Well, how about some fishing? Holly, why don't you try first? Maybe you'll have good luck."

She cast only a few times before she had a strike. By the time we reached her with the net, she'd flipped the fish out of the water, a big fish, with iridescent spots all along its shimmering skin. It struggled on the gravel bank, alive and frantic, the way we'd feel if we were drowning. It *was* drowning. In air. Not in an ice-cold river, but drowning just the same.

Suddenly I felt sick to my stomach, panicky. I shivered. "It's suffering!" I cried. "Kill it quick."

Michael looked at me, his eyes wide, but to my amazement he didn't laugh. My friends would have laughed at what I had just said. But Michael didn't. Instead he raced down the bank, grabbed a rock and smashed the fish on the head. It quit struggling.

I took a deep breath. "Poor thing," I said awkwardly.

"It's nature." Dad's voice was soft, his face concerned. "Living things kill other living things to eat. That's how the tuna got in the can."

Michael picked up the dead fish and carried it to the edge of the lake to clean it. With a single slit of his sharp knife, he opened the bright pink flesh of its belly. The fish's tiny sharp teeth grimaced, exposed and useless in death.

"What kind of fish is it?" I asked.

"Cutthroat trout," Michael answered, scooping its intestines into the lake. The coils hung suspended in the clear water as though in air. "Its flesh is pink from eating tiny shrimp," he said. "You'll be surprised how good this fish tastes. Because of the shrimp and such cold water."

I put my hand in the lake and pulled it back immediately. The water felt so icy my fingers tingled.

"I've got one!" Dad yelled. He flipped the trembling frantic thing onto the gravel bank, then bent to hit it on the head. A smaller fish but just as beautiful. We'd soon have enough for supper if this kept up. Dad handed his rod to me. "Greg, your turn."

"No, I don't feel like it." I kept seeing that fish flipping, slapping at the rocks. I'd seen hundreds of fish caught. What was wrong with me today? I used to catch fish myself when I was a little kid. Just because I'd fallen in the river didn't mean I should be acting like a wimp.

One afternoon years before, when our family was on a picnic, Mom had said she felt sorry for the poor fish we caught. We had all laughed at her, even Michael. She'd gone for a long walk by herself then.

But this time Michael hadn't laughed.

My brother picked up his fishing rod and handed it to Holly again. "Try for another one."

"I think I'll go for a walk. Around the lake." She smiled at him, and suddenly I knew I hadn't been mistaken. Those weren't just "friendship" eyes.

I sat down on a big rock and watched her walk away, across the thick gravel. Michael cast a few times, then propped his rod against a boulder and headed after Holly.

"Where are you going, Michael?" Dad asked. "What happened to my fishing partner?"

"I'm going for a walk too."

"What's wrong with all you guys today?" Dad shook his head and cast again.

Twenty

*M*ichael caught up to Holly. I watched them as they walked together, talking, smiling, gazing into each other's eyes, then looking up to the mountain and back to the lake. They weren't holding hands yet, but they were walking very close.

When they came to the first big snowbank, they climbed to the top and slid over the snow down toward the lake, using their boots like skis, balancing to keep upright, howling with laughter. The snow sparkled in the sunlight like a million diamonds.

I watched as about halfway down Holly fell and Michael tumbled beside her. Laughing, they helped each other up and climbed to the top again. This time they made it all the way, skidding sideways to stop at the edge of the lake. Over and over they slid down that snowbank, giggling like children.

It looked fun. I knew if I joined them, they wouldn't think I was in the way. I wanted to try it. Skiing in July on a snowbank by a turquoise lake at the top of the world. Skiing in only my boots, playing in warm sunlight, laughing with them.

Michael looked happier than I'd ever seen him. Didn't my brother have a right to be happy? Why not join them? It could be something great that we did together. Making good memories, Holly called it.

But before I stood up, they'd finished with that game and continued around the lake, walking closer than before, tilting their heads toward each other to talk. Then they were holding hands. I could hardly swallow. My chest felt tight.

They walked on. But now they were both looking straight ahead, and didn't seem to be talking, caught at that stage of awkwardness that comes from a scary new closeness. Within a few minutes, though, I could see they were looking at each other again as they strolled on around the lake. Dad was right. The lake was much bigger than it looked. Michael and Holly seemed small now, faraway, dwarfed by the huge mountain. I couldn't keep my eyes off them.

"Got another one!" Dad flipped a fish onto the bank. "It's huge." I couldn't believe Dad hadn't even noticed his youngest son walking hand in hand with a girl.

As Dad took the fish off the hook, it gave a mighty lurch and flopped down the bank. "Grab the net!" he shouted. I obeyed and scooped the fish up just before it hit the water. "Thanks, Greg. You did great."

The fish lurched again. I pulled the wet silky creature out of the net, grabbed a rock and smashed its head. It quivered once more, then lay still.

Dad glanced over toward Michael and Holly from the corner of his eye, then looked quickly back at me.

Oh, yes, he sure did know. "Don't you want to try, Greg? When you were young, you used to love fishing."

"I really don't feel like it today."

Dad nodded. Suddenly I wondered what else he understood.

"I'm going for a walk," I said.

"Everybody's going for a walk. Must be catching." He smiled. But his eyes looked sad.

Holly and Michael were at the far side of the lake now, climbing along a steep gravel slope. I headed for the bank they had skied on. Once there, I sat on a rock staring at the long parallel skid lines etched into the white surface. Suddenly, I didn't feel like "boot skiing" anymore. I picked up a handful of the heavy wet stuff — packing snow, the kind we loved to use for snowballs and snowmen when we were little kids.

I formed a snowball, packed it hard and whipped it into the lake. It shattered the mirror surface, leaving a widening circle of colored ripples.

Holly should be back looking for Patches. What was she doing wandering around the lake gazing at Michael? I choked, detesting the feeling that tore through my insides. I formed a larger ball. Then I came up with the crazy idea of building a snowman. Why not? A snowman in July. So I started rolling the ball around. Layer after layer of soft wet snow stuck to it until I had a huge sphere big enough for his tummy. Another made his chest. By then the knees of my jeans were soaking wet and my bare hands were red and numb from the icy snow, but I didn't care.

I looked up and saw Holly and Michael coming back.

I rolled another sphere to make my snowman's head. He was almost as tall as I was. A few pebbles gave him buttons, a mouth and eyes. A couple of branches from a bush in the ravine made his arms. A piece of twig formed his long crooked nose.

Holly and Michael were almost back to me and I could see them grinning at my creation. As they approached, I took off my cowboy hat and put it on the round white head. It tilted over one eye giving the snowman a funny, wicked look.

Holly's eyes were sparkling. "He's great. A snowman in July." She pretended to shake his hand. "Hello, sir. How are you?" She laughed. "We should have a picture of him. Now where's your camera, Michael?"

"I'll be right back." He scrambled off to get it.

Holly stood looking at my snowman. Then she turned to the lake. "Greg, I've never seen a place so heavenly. I would have hated to miss this."

"Miss what?" I growled.

"This." She spread her arms to the mountains and the sky, breathing deeply, smiling broadly.

"It looked to me like you were too busy with Michael to notice the scenery."

"What's that supposed to mean?"

"It sure didn't take you long to fall for my brother. He must be quite the guy."

"Yeah, maybe he is." Her voice sounded tight. She made a snowball and flung it into the lake. "You just can't stand to see anybody appreciate Michael, can you? If I liked anybody else in the world but Michael it wouldn't bother you at all."

I rearranged the pebble buttons on my snowman.

Holly pushed her glasses up. "Michael is sixteen years old. Don't you ever want him to have a girlfriend?"

"You said you were just interested in him as a friend."

She looked away. "Haven't you ever changed how you felt about anything?"

My hands were shaking. Probably because they were so cold from the snow. I shoved them into my pockets. "What happened to all your noble talk about not spoiling beautiful friendships?"

"I said I've seen it happen in lots of cases. But some people stay friends even if they're, uh, more than friends."

Michael was standing beside Dad, handing him his camera. I felt frantic. "Holly, I thought you were different from all the other boy-crazy girls."

"Oh, now you don't want *me* to be interested in anybody! Boys and girls do fall for each other. It isn't anything new, in case you haven't heard. And I don't see why it matters to you."

If only I could tell her. I sneered. "How come you were so sure yesterday morning that you just wanted to be friends with Michael? You didn't want anything to happen that would hurt him."

"How come you're so worried about your brother all of a sudden?" She clasped and unclasped her hands. "You can still be friends with someone even when you . . . are interested in them in a different way."

"Is that related to 'You can still love someone even when you don't always like them'?" I glared at her. "You're great at coming up with these stupid sayings."

She made another snowball and moved it slowly from hand to hand. Michael was talking to Dad now. Soon he'd be back. I swallowed, wishing I could force my dry mouth to say something neutral that would stop this terrible conversation. If I kept this up, Holly would hate me. I couldn't stand that.

Holly dropped the snowball. "Michael really cares about *you*, Greg. Why can't you let him be happy about something?"

"I'm sure you're not really in love with him," I snarled. "Probably it's just hormones. Or maybe you just want to see how hard you can make him fall so you can walk away and leave him to pick up the pieces . . ."

I had pushed her too far. She turned abruptly and headed toward Michael and Dad. I followed her, unable to stop myself. She walked faster.

"Holly, I'm sorry."

She was almost running.

"Holly, please. I didn't mean those things. None of them. Holly . . ."

Both Michael and Dad were walking our way now. And although they couldn't have heard what we'd been saying, it would be obvious that Holly wasn't pleased about something.

Within a couple of minutes she had reached Michael. "What's wrong?" my brother asked her.

She put her hand in his, her lip trembled, but she forced a smile and said, "Oh, we were having a little disagreement. You know how I like to argue about things."

Michael's eyes narrowed. He looked at me, but didn't ask anything more.

"What about the picture?" Dad asked. "I was going to take a picture of you three and the snowman."

We followed Dad to the snowman. He posed us and took a couple of shots, capturing forever my snowman in July and our plastic pasted-on smiles.

Twenty-One

Dad handed the camera back to Michael. "Maybe he's in camp now," my father said. "Holly, you'd better get back there."

"Keep your fingers crossed," she murmured, looking up at Michael with soft eyes as he touched her hand.

Stupid lovesick puppies! I kicked my snowman over. He lay decapitated, his head nearby with gray pebble eyes staring blindly at the sky. I spun around and headed up the narrow trail that led above the lake, the trail that Michael and I had followed together to the north valley.

Dad was the one to break the shocked silence. "Greg!" I kept climbing. "Greg!" he called again.

I needed to escape. Gulping air, my heart hammering, I climbed higher and higher. The pain eased a bit as my muscles and lungs struggled to get me up the mountainside. Stopping to catch my breath, I looked down. It was hard to believe how high I had come. Everybody looked small and faraway. Dad was sitting on a boulder. Holly and Michael were strolling along the shore toward camp, walking close. They looked ridiculous together. He was almost twice as tall as Holly and only half as wide.

I kept climbing, following the trail around the side of the mountain until Sky Lake disappeared from view. At last I was alone. And I was surprised to discover that being by myself could actually feel less lonely than being with people.

Soon I'd be at the little meadow with the bubbling spring and the tiny creek. My throat yearned for a drink of that sweet spring water.

When I got to the meadow, I was amazed to see five bighorn sheep grazing, all rams with huge curled horns. They lifted their heads and stared for a moment, then trotted ahead of me on the trail going north. But a little farther around the hill, they turned off the trail onto an even narrower path that led over the rocks, up and along the curve of the mountain.

I followed the sheep, hardly daring to breathe. It felt good to have something to think about other than the mess I'd just left down by the lake. As we climbed, the sheep slowed down and seemed to relax.

They hadn't yet finished shedding their shaggy winter coats. Lumpy mats of beige hair hung in shreds from their bellies and between their legs. Still, they looked noble, moving smoothly, making their climb seem effortless.

The trail became just a track worn into the loose sharp shale in the shadow of a long granite wall. The mountain sheep were walking more slowly, confident now I was not going to hurt them. Their white fluffy rumps moved in rhythm. Their tiny hooves clicked softly as they leapt from rock to rock, nimble as gymnasts.

I kept thinking of my brother walking hand in hand with Holly. What did Michael have going for him? If I really tried, surely I could make Holly forget about him.

Past the wall, the trail became much worse — only about as wide as my hand along the thick layer of loose sharp rocks. A horse would never be able to manage it. Dare I try? One of the sheep glanced back at me, then kept climbing.

I placed my feet carefully, but several rocks started sliding, gathering momentum, pushing other rocks along. There was nothing to hang on to. I looked down the side of the mountain, my head spinning. The rams moved on. The higher we went, the more relaxed they seemed.

I zipped up my jacket as the wind sharpened, icy and raw. I knew I should turn around. The rams passed a couple of moss pinks. I stopped to smell them for Holly's sake, and thought again of roses and how Linda had chased me so much I came to dread the sight of her. If I chased Holly when she didn't want me, she'd come to hate me the same way.

Finding a footing became even harder as I watched the rams stroll out of sight again, but I kept following them, disgusted with myself. The trail was really awful now.

Then I turned the corner and gasped at what I saw. The rams were in a tiny sheltered alcove at the very edge of a rock precipice. I stood only a few steps from five wild animals, but not one of them moved.

They were lying down, all except the biggest who stood proudly like a king, as though guarding the others. He was staring at me, his eyes cool and level. On both sides of his head tremendous horns curved almost full circle.

All five of the mountain sheep had been watching when I rounded the corner, and not one of them had taken his eyes off me yet. Above the alcove a steep cliff rose toward the sheer gray side of Barricade Mountain. I looked down and was surprised to see a tiny pool far below us, a shiny turquoise circle of water, and beside it, a minute patch of green grass and wildflowers.

The temperature was dropping and the wind became stronger. Just a few more steps and I could be in the sheep's alcove. I chuckled at the idea. "Somehow I don't think you guys would appreciate me trying to crawl in there with you," I said, keeping my voice low.

The sheep had trusted me enough to lead me to their secret place. It felt good to be trusted, like when Michael had trusted me enough to tell how he felt about Holly. I had betrayed his trust by making fun of those feelings. My stomach knotted just thinking about it.

A dark cloud was building behind Barricade Mountain. I had to start back! But I sat down on one of the rocks, unable to leave, feeling as though I'd found something I needed.

Would Holly have caught Patches by now? Would Michael and Holly be hugging each other, thrilled, gazing into each other's eyes? Somehow, thinking about that didn't hurt quite as much up here.

Oh, for a camera! This scene would make the best picture in the world. The five sheep so close, the tiny pool, the sharp precipice, the grass and brilliantly colored flowers below.

The sheep were still watching me. I'd have given anything for a camera. But, no, pictures usually turned out disappointing, flat, not like the real thing. Maybe it was good I didn't have a camera here. I'd never be able to describe this scene to anyone, either. Words would dilute it and make it flat like a photo. This was mine. Only mine.

I took a deep breath and leaned back to stretch my arms, drinking in every detail. Lines in the rock around the cove, the jagged broken edge on one of the ram's horns, the tiny crisp wine-colored flower in front of their hiding place, a hawk hanging in the air above the cliff, fighting the force of the wind.

The bighorns didn't feel the wind in their shelter. Five guys huddling together. So close. Good friends. I wondered if any of them were brothers. Or maybe half-brothers.

I was surprised to find myself wishing Michael could be here to see this, too. He'd appreciate it more than anyone I knew. It seemed almost sad not to be able to share this with somebody, especially a brother who would really understand.

It was starting to rain. I had to go back immediately. The rocks would be slippery on the way down. The trail was already dangerous enough.

I pulled myself up and forced my legs to move, one careful step at a time, over the loose shale, then turned for one last look at my five friends. They were still watching me. Rocks teetered under my feet as I worked my way down, arms out for balance, mouth dry, willing myself not to look when a piece of shale tumbled over the drop-off.

Then I was around the edge of their slope and knew I'd never see those sheep again. But I'd never forget them, either. Would they remember me? A year or two years from now, would they remember the strange two-legged creature who had followed them up the side of their mountain and sat for an endless time matching gazes with them?

I struggled over the slippery rocks, down and around the side of the ridge. Despite the frightening trail, I was filled with a kind of peace. I, too, had found something in this crazy week to take home. Maybe beautiful memories could help shelter a person through messes or turmoil, if only you could figure out how to use them.

"Greg! Greg!"

My mind was playing tricks on me. I could hear the wind calling my name. The rain was cold and sharp. I wished for my raincoat. The path became more and more slippery.

"Greg!"

It sounded like Michael's voice. I stopped. It *was* Michael's voice. I could hear him call, muffled, from somewhere below.

"Michael! I'm here!" The wind swallowed my words. I shouted louder. "Michael!"

"Greg! Where are you?"

"Up here!" I shouted. A few steps more and I could see them, Michael and Holly, headed *away* from me along the main trail, following the echo of my voice from across the valley.

"Greg! Where are you?" Michael called again.

What were they doing up here? Probably they had come to tell me the good news. That Holly had caught her horse and now we could go home. Again and again I hollered. Finally they turned, waved and started climbing toward me. Step by step I maneuvered down the sheep's path, placing my feet cautiously over the sliding shale.

I could see Holly gasping for breath, her face flushed, wet hair hanging in her eyes. Michael didn't look too bad. His jogging had paid off.

"Did you get him?" I called as they approached.

They shook their heads. "No sign of him yet," Holly said. "Maybe this rain will bring him into camp to shelter under the big trees."

I turned my head to hide my disappointment.

"Greg, what's wrong?" My brother looked worried. "How come you kicked over your snowman? Why did you get mad? Is it anything we did?" asked Michael, putting his arm around Holly's shoulder.

She leaned toward him. "Greg, please tell us what's wrong," Holly said, her face worried too. Obviously neither of them had any idea how I felt about her.

Without speaking, I moved past them down the steep trail, going too fast, trying to get away. Rocks slid at the touch of my boots. Michael scrambled close behind me. "Greg, what's wrong?"

"Nothing."

"Something sure is."

My bootlace felt loose. I bent to retie it. Michael and Holly stood close together, waiting. Glancing back at them, I lost my balance. The shale started to slide. I stuck my foot out, skidding to a stop, then bent much more carefully to finish tying the lace.

"Here, lean on me," Michael said, putting his arm out.

"Get away," I yelled, and swung my fist at him. He ducked. I caught a glimpse of the terror in his eyes as my momentum carried me off the trail. The heavy layer of loose shale started sliding, pulling me down with it. My left foot twisted under my weight. I crumpled to the ground.

Pain throbbed through my ankle, but even worse, Holly was glaring at me. I couldn't stand for her to look at me that way. Then she spoke, her voice as cold as the river. "What kind of person would hit his brother when he was just trying to help?"

I looked down the steep mountainside and wished I had kept sliding right to the bottom, to the boulders far below. It had been so good watching the mountain sheep. Now suddenly everything had gone wrong.

The temperature was dropping rapidly, rain turning to snow. Huge wet flakes hurtled at us. I couldn't sit there forever. Michael stared down at me, his eyes still wide with fear.

Holly worked her way toward me. "See if you can stand." She reached her arm under mine and pulled. I stood, then took a couple of steps, wincing, but relieved I could put weight on that ankle. At least it wasn't sprained! Together we scrambled up the steep loose shale. Back on the path, Holly stood, struggling for breath.

I took another few steps down the trail, putting as

much weight as possible on my good foot, still feeling the place Holly's arm had been around my waist.

"Now listen to me, Greg Kepler," she said, puffing. "Somebody has to help you over this trail or you'll really hurt that ankle. Michael's stronger and fitter than I am, so it's going to be him, whether you like it or not."

"It's okay," I snapped. "I can make it on my own."

"Why would I try to help him again?" Michael said. "He'd just knock me off the mountain. I don't care if he dies up here."

Holly glared at Michael, then back to me, her mouth trembling. "That's it! I've had enough of you two! I'm going back down to find my horse. And you can stay up here forever, both of you, as far as I'm concerned."

Silently we watched her scramble down the slippery path, then disappear around the edge of the slope. I was still standing, my sore foot barely resting on the ground. Michael came toward me unsmiling, an arm outstretched.

"It's okay," I said again. "I can do it on my own." I started along the path, letting my good foot do as much work as possible.

Michael glowered at me, his jaw set. Then without a word, he turned and walked ahead, his back straight, his stride more and more rapid.

Twenty-Two

I watched my brother leave, and felt terror. I was losing something. Something I needed. It was Holly's fault. Just for a moment I choked with resentment toward her. Holly had come between Michael and me.

When we'd found Patches two days before, my brother and I had hugged each other and laughed together. But we had lost that feeling. All because of Holly.

No. I gulped and shook my head. No. It wasn't her fault. And if I kept acting this way, both Michael and Holly would detest me. My insides churned just thinking about it.

A large piece of shale slid under my foot, and down I went again. Michael swung around and retraced his steps. "Lean on me, you idiot. Let me help you." He had never talked to me like that before.

"The path isn't wide enough for two. It's dangerous for you to walk beside me."

"So?" he growled. Then he put his hands under my arms, pulled me up and raised his shoulder to take my weight as we headed down the trail. The wind was sharp now, snow hurling at us, thick and fast, cutting into our faces.

I could have got down alone. I'd already made it over the worst of the trail. But it felt good to take the weight off my sore foot, like finding shelter in a storm. I thought of the five rams huddled together in their alcove. Life was simple for them. Or was it? They had hunger, hunters, all kinds of problems.

Finally we came to the long granite wall, then around the curve, and we were back out into the open. The wind had died down. Over the next hill was the little meadow where I'd first seen the sheep.

Would Holly be in camp yet? Maybe Patches would be there too. Tomorrow Duke would carry me back to the real world. The real world. It seemed like ages since we'd left it.

My ankle was still sore, but with Michael bearing most of my weight on that side, I hardly needed to touch my toe to the ground. Thanks, Michael, I wanted to say. Thanks for seeing me through all this even when I'm being awful to you. I needed to thank him. But the words stuck in my throat.

Instead I said, "Michael, I followed five mountain sheep. Big rams with curled horns."

"Where?"

"Way up there, around the far edge of that slope. They led me to their hiding place, high above a tiny turquoise pool. I sat so close to them. They were lying down, but they didn't move, just stared at me."

"You lucky guy!"

"Wanna hear a crazy thing?" I laughed. "I was wishing you were there with me. So you could see them, too."

He didn't answer, only beamed. I could feel his tense back relax. My muscles relaxed too.

We walked on then, not talking, balancing together on the slippery teetering rocks. I leaned on him harder and he took the weight. We moved along almost in step. We were just above the little meadow where we could have a drink of clear fresh spring water — if we wanted to kneel in the snow.

My ankle was hardly hurting anymore. I really could make it on my own, but it felt good to have my brother's support over the treacherous path. For such a skinny guy, he was amazingly strong.

The snow was falling gently now, so thick we could hardly see. On we hobbled, in a strangely cozy world of silent white. Then I spotted something dark below us. I peered through the snow. Suddenly I realized what I was seeing. A horse, grazing at the sheltered side of the little meadow!

My heart thumped. "Michael, we've just found Patches."

At the sound of my voice, the old pinto looked up, then bent his head to graze again. He wouldn't worry about us when we were this far away as long as we spoke quietly.

I couldn't believe how easy it was going to be. In a few more minutes Holly would be able to catch her horse.

"Michael," I said, my voice low, "we can herd him

along the trail right into camp." Holly would be there. I thought of how she'd smile when she saw him coming toward her.

"No," my brother said, "*I* need to . . . *We* need to catch him."

"Are you crazy?" I hissed. "Here we are so close to getting this horse to Holly, and you want to complicate things so you can be the big hero and catch him yourself!"

"Don't you understand?" he asked, his eyes boring into mine, pleading.

I forgot all about being quiet. "No way!" I yelled.

Patches looked up and snorted.

"Okay," I said more softly, taking a deep breath. "You win this one. But let's not make a habit of it."

My thoughts were racing. Somehow we could figure this out. Like solving a math problem. There were no trees here and no ropes. But there had to be a way.

I wasn't much good with my sore ankle. Couldn't run over the rocks, that's for sure, all because of that blasted loose shale . . .

"That's it!" I said, trying to keep from shouting with excitement. "The shale!"

Michael stared at me.

"The shale," I said. "He won't be able to walk off the path in the shale. He'd slide and slip if he even tried. Just like I did, only worse because he's a big old heavy horse."

Still, Michael stared at me.

I was so excited it was hard to talk sensibly. "You go down to the main trail. Around the hill. He can't see when you reach the fork. Pile up some rocks to block off the main trail so he can't go north. It's narrow. It won't take a lot of rocks."

"Why would he want to go north when I'm there?"

"You won't be. You're going to sneak around up the hill, back to the south side of the little meadow, and head him away from camp along the main trail. But it'll be blocked, so he'll have to turn up this sheep path."

Michael's eyes lit up. "You really aren't as dumb as you look."

I smiled. "Meanwhile, I'll climb back up by the rock wall to hide. When he comes along this trail I'll reach out and grab his rope."

"Sounds too easy," Michael said. "So easy it worries me."

"Well, we could have a big fight and mess it all up . . ."

Michael laughed. "It's okay, we'll manage without the fight this time. Wish me luck."

He headed down the hill. It was getting harder to see through the snow. I limped back up the slippery trail, grateful that the wind had calmed down. It wouldn't do to fall again.

Finally I reached the rock wall. All I could see was white. I knew the edge fell straight down below me just a few meters on the other side of the path. I waited, leaning against the cold granite. In the silence my heart pounded. Then came the sound of rocks hitting each other. Michael was stacking them to make the barrier across the main path. What if the noise scared Patches? Naw, it wouldn't. Patches was on the other side of the hill. The sound would be muffled from there.

Silence again. Total silence. Forever, it seemed. My

ankle was hurting but I couldn't sit down on the cold wet snow. Then at last I heard it, the clacking of metal horseshoes over loose rock, coming closer and closer. Without thinking, I peered around the wall and almost choked because Patches was much closer than I thought.

The instant he saw me he swerved off the path into the loose shale. He jerked his head around, struggled desperately to keep his footing as the rocks shifted. But he fell and started sliding down the mountain, his legs thrashing in the tumbling shale.

I watched, sick to my stomach. Michael, too, stood paralyzed. As Patches' hooves scrambled more and more frantically, the rock slide carried him even faster toward the precipice.

"Whoa," Michael bellowed. And Patches stopped struggling. Instantly. It was as though he had already realized that struggling was making things worse and the familiar word showed him what he needed to do. He was smart all right. He knew a good idea when he heard one.

The rocks slid a bit more, a couple of them bouncing off the ledge. We could hear them echo as they hit bottom, way below the drop-off. But Patches lay absolutely still until the shale had stopped sliding. Then carefully, gently, he pulled himself to a standing position, freezing each time the rocks started to shift again. One footstep after the other, pausing the instant the rocks started sliding, that old horse climbed back up the loose shale to the mountain sheep's path.

He swung his head, looking from Michael on the path below him to me on the path above him. You could see he knew when he was trapped. No way was he going back down into that shale!

He stood facing me, his head low, his long straight eyelashes blinking against the heavy snow. "Good boy," I cooed, easing toward him. Carefully I grabbed his halter rope and reached out to scratch the old horse's nose.

His face glowing, Michael crept up beside Patches. "Here, you take him," I said, handing the halter rope to my brother.

Sometimes happiness is too deep for words. That's how it was. We didn't say anything, just headed down the trail together, Michael leading Patches and supporting me through the falling snow. I thought of climbing on Patches for the ride down, but his back was soaking wet.

We reached the main trail and together, with Michael still holding Patches' rope, we dismantled the rock barrier. Then the three of us headed down the path toward camp. My foot was hardly hurting at all now, but still I leaned on Michael. "That ankle might mess you up for dancing tomorrow night," he said.

"Aw, there'll be other parties." I gulped, trying to ease the pain in my throat.

Again we were silent. Just the sound of Patches' hooves on the rocks behind us.

Then Michael spoke, so softly at first that I thought I was imagining it. "Greg . . ."

"Yeah?"

"Greg, could you tell me what you and Holly were talking about down there by the snowman?"

"Oh, nothing."

"I got the feeling it was something really important. Please, could you tell me?"

I took a deep breath. "We were talking about . . . liking and not liking, and friendship and brothers. Things like that."

Michael was staring at me, but I couldn't raise my eyes. We walked another couple of steps. "Greg . . ." His voice sounded thin and scared. "Greg, you wouldn't be interested in Holly, would you?"

I looked away, hesitated almost too long. "What gave you that dumb idea?"

Sometimes you can't have everything, I told myself. But my chest had never ached thinking about any other girl before. What had she done to me? I closed my eyes trying to shut out the pain. Holly didn't want me. If I chased her, she'd soon dread the sight of me. Trying to come between Michael and Holly would make my brother hate me, too. I had to give up wanting her or lose both of them.

Michael stopped and watched me, his eyes narrowed. Then he said slowly, "She really deserves somebody good-looking and popular like you — a lot more than she deserves an ugly crazy guy like me."

"Sorry." I laughed too loudly. "You know she's not my type!"

Still watching my face, he hesitated, then said, "Greg, if you were interested in her, I would never come between the two of you. Because you might hate me for it. And I need a brother as much as I need a girlfriend. Maybe more."

Why didn't I just admit how I felt about her? But I

needed a brother too. And Holly had chosen Michael, not me.

Michael must never know how I felt about Holly. Never. And somehow, in time, the pain would ease away.

The wind had picked up again. I held my hand over my eyes to shelter them from the stinging snow. "You say you need a brother?" My voice sounded a bit shaky. "And maybe Holly needs one, too. So I guess I have quite a job cut out for me."

I turned to look at the old horse trudging along behind us and thought of a little boy sitting on the steps with a clump of wilted dandelions in his hands. There was something I had to know. "Michael, does the name Jonathan mean anything to you?"

I watched for his reaction. His forehead creased and he concentrated a few seconds before answering. "I don't think so. Should it?"

She had never told him about Jonathan! In all the time she'd known him, in all the hours they'd ridden horses together, she had never told Michael about her brother. But she had told me. Realizing that sent a shiver along my spine. Maybe I really was close to her in a special way. Like a brother.

To be a brother to someone was important too. You have to give up some things, I told myself, but what you find instead could be worth even more. And eventually pain always stops.

"Who is Jonathan?" asked Michael.

"Oh, somebody's brother."

"Whose?"

"Uh, you know. David and Jonathan. From the Bible story. They were real friends, like brothers . . ."

He was staring at me, puzzled.

I had to change the subject. Raising my hands into the howling wind and snow, I lifted my head, and in a dramatic Shakespearean voice, declared, "'So foul and fair a day I have not seen.'"

Grinning at his wide shocked eyes, I leaned against my brother, and with Patches following us, we hobbled on through the storm.